Fair Play

"Martin depicts the worlds of both professional hockey and ethnic Brooklyn with deftness and smart detail. She has an unerring eye for humorous family dynamics [and] sweet buoyancy." —*Publishers Weekly*

"Fast-paced, wisecracking, and an enjoyable story . . . Makes you feel like you're flying." —*Rendezvous*

"A fun and witty story . . . The depth of characterizations and the unexpectedly moving passages make this an exceptional romance and a must-read for all fans of the genre." —*Booklist*

"A fine sports romance that will score big-time . . . Martin has provided a winner." —*Midwest Book Review*

"Sure to delight both fans of professional ice hockey and those who enjoy a good romance." —*Affaire de Coeur*

continued . . .

Body Check

"Heartwarming." —*Booklist*

"Combines sports and romance in a way that reminded me of Susan Elizabeth Phillips's *It Had To Be You*, but Deirdre Martin has her own style and voice. *Body Check* is one of the best first novels I have read in a long time."

—*All About Romance*
(Desert Island Keeper)

"Deirdre Martin aims for the net and scores with *Body Check*." —*The Romance Reader*
(Four Hearts)

"You don't have to be a hockey fan to cheer for *Body Check*. Deirdre Martin brings readers a story that scores."

—*The Word On Romance*

"Fun, fast-paced, and sexy, *Body Check* is a dazzling debut." —Millie Criswell, *USA Today* bestselling author of *Mad About Mia*

"Fun, delightful, emotional, and sexy, *Body Check* is an utterly enthralling, fast-paced novel. This is one author I eagerly look forward to reading more from."

—*Romance Reviews Today*

"An engaging romance that scores a hat trick [with] a fine supporting cast." —*The Best Reviews*

Be sure to visit the Blades' website at
www.nyblades.com

TOTAL RUSH

Deirdre Martin

BERKLEY SENSATION, NEW YORK

THE BERKLEY PUBLISHING GROUP
Published by the Penguin Group
Penguin Group (USA) Inc.
375 Hudson Street, New York, New York 10014, USA
Penguin Group (Canada), 10 Alcorn Avenue, Toronto, Ontario M4V 3B2, Canada
(a division of Pearson Penguin Canada Inc.)
Penguin Books Ltd., 80 Strand, London WC2R 0RL, England
Penguin Group Ireland, 25 St. Stephen's Green, Dublin 2, Ireland (a division of Penguin Books Ltd.)
Penguin Group (Australia), 250 Camberwell Road, Camberwell, Victoria 3124, Australia
(a division of Pearson Australia Group Pty. Ltd.)
Penguin Books India Pvt. Ltd., 11 Community Centre, Panchsheel Park, New Delhi—110 017, India
Penguin Group (NZ), Cnr. Airborne and Rosedale Roads, Albany, Auckland 1310, New Zealand
(a division of Pearson New Zealand Ltd.)
Penguin Books (South Africa) (Pty.) Ltd., 24 Sturdee Avenue, Rosebank, Johannesburg 2196,
South Africa

Penguin Books Ltd., Registered Offices: 80 Strand, London WC2R 0RL, England

This is a work of fiction. Names, characters, places, and incidents either are the product of the author's imagination or are used fictitiously, and any resemblance to actual persons, living or dead, business establishments, events, or locales is entirely coincidental.

TOTAL RUSH

A Berkley Sensation Book / published by arrangement with the author

PRINTING HISTORY
Berkley Sensation edition / March 2005

ISBN: 978-0-425-20152-7

BERKLEY® SENSATION
Berkley Sensation Books are published by The Berkley Publishing Group,
a division of Penguin Group (USA) Inc.,
375 Hudson Street, New York, New York 10014.
BERKLEY SENSATION and the "B" design are trademarks belonging to Penguin Group (USA) Inc.

PRINTED IN THE UNITED STATES OF AMERICA

10 9 8 7 6 5

For my sister Allison,
with gratitude for her love and friendship

Special thanks to

Lt. Dave Burbank and Lt. Gillian Sharp of the Ithaca Fire Department, whose willingness to take me inside their world helped make this book possible. Also firefighter Rob Covert, my CISD source.

Lt. John Miles of Ladder 35/Engine 40 in Manhattan, for allowing me to see how it's done in the big city and answering my endless questions without complaint.

Assistant Fire Chief Mike Schnurle, Mark Spadolini, Wade Bardo, Dan Zajak, and anyone else I might have missed from IFD's "D" shift. Your hospitality and friendliness made all the difference in the world to me.

The firefighters of Ladder 35/Engine 40 in Manhattan.

Thanks also to

My husband, Mark Levine, for his incredible patience.

Roberta Caploe, for allowing me to put her gorgeous apartment in three books.

Ken Dashow, for putting me in touch with Lt. John Miles.

Maggie Shayne.

Rachel Dickinson.

Dr. Brian Carpenter.

Elaine English and Allison McCabe.

And last but not least, Mom, Dad, Bill, Allison, Beth, Jane, Dave, and Tom, who, along with Mark and "the lads," make everything worthwhile.

CHAPTER

01

"I need your help."

Looking up, Gemma Dante smiled as her cousin Michael came bounding to the counter of the Golden Bough. As usual, the cozy, welcoming bookstore in Greenwich Village was filled with customers, some browsing among the bookshelves, others lounging in one of the plump armchairs Gemma provided. Soft Celtic music played, while the faint scent of lavender incense filled the air. The sense of serenity had no effect on Michael Dante, however. Right winger for the New York Blades, he was a man always in a hurry, both on the ice and off.

Gemma stepped out from behind the counter to give her cousin an affectionate hug. "'I need your help,'" she repeated. "I think I'll have that carved on my tombstone." People instinctively came to her for aid and advice—not that she minded. She enjoyed playing the part of an offbeat Ann Landers to friends and family.

"Tombstone?" Michael feigned surprise. "I always figured when you went, you'd have some kind of moonlight ceremony where you'd be transformed into fairy dust and returned to the cosmos."

"Remember that old Squeeze song that begins, 'If I didn't love you, I'd hate you'? I think of you every time I hear it, Mikey."

"And I think of you every time I hear Donovan's 'Season of the Witch.'" He glanced around the store. "Not too many freaks today."

Gemma ignored the crack, returning to her post behind the cash register. "What can I do for you?"

"There's this new guy on the team, Ron Crabnutt. He was just called up from Rochester and he doesn't know a soul in the city apart from us guys. He's dying to go out with a 'real New York woman.' So I thought maybe—if you had time—you could break bread with him one night this week."

Gemma looked dubious. "Are you trying to set me up on a date?"

"No, no, no," Michael swore. "Well—yeah. It's an act of kindness, you know? For someone who's new to town."

"I thought I was too 'weird' for your teammates."

Michael snorted. "You're too good for them! If you saw some of the skanks these guys hung out with . . ." He shuddered.

"Good to know I'm one up on the skanks, Mikey."

He rounded the counter and gave her a bone-crushing squeeze. "Will you do it? He's a really nice guy, Gem, cross my heart. And who knows? Maybe you two will hit it off." He winked.

Gemma chuckled. "I'm not looking for a boyfriend."

"A relationship would be good for you."

Gemma changed the subject. "Speaking of relationships, how's Theresa? The baby?"

Michael smiled giddily. "Both doing great. The christening invitations just went out in the mail. You're coming, right?"

"Are you kidding? I wouldn't miss it for the world."

"Good. And Crabnutt? You'll have dinner with him?"

Gemma shrugged. "Okay. What have I got to lose? It might be fun."

"I knew I could count on you!"

"That'll be the second line on my tombstone."

Goddess, why did I let Mikey talk me into this? Gemma thought, struggling to keep her eyes from glazing over. She had agreed to do this as a favor, and because it might fun. Little did she know she'd be listening to someone drone on ecstatically about his screwdriver collection.

"Now, your clutchhead tips have four points of contact—"

"Excuse me," she interrupted Ron Crabnutt politely. "Could we talk about something other than screwdrivers?"

"Sure." Ron looked wounded. "What would you like to talk about?"

"How about politics?"

"Well, I gotta be honest with you . . ." A mild grimace tugged at Crabnutt's lower lip. "I don't really give a monkey's hinder about politics."

Gemma blinked. *Monkey's hinder?* "How about music, then?"

Ron's face lit up. "You like Skid Row?"

"Skid Row?"

"Don't tell me you've never heard of Skid Row!" Ron exclaimed, smacking the table in disbelief. "They're only the greatest band EVER."

Maybe talking about screwdrivers wasn't so bad after all. "I'm more into Celtic music myself. Solas, Loreena McKennitt . . ."

"Never heard of 'em," Ron grumbled. "If it doesn't make your teeth rattle, I don't want to know."

Gemma deflated. "Right." She decided to give it one

more try. Perhaps a conversational push in the right direction would reveal unimagined depth to his personality. "Do you have any hobbies besides the screwdrivers?" she asked.

"Other hobbies." Ron peered hard at his fork. "Hhmm."

The longer he took to answer, the more Gemma knew the only depth she'd be exploring would be that of her own despair.

"I like gum," Ron offered hopefully.

Gum, Gemma thought desperately. *I can work with that.*

"Collecting it or chewing it?"

"Chewing." Ron bobbed his head thoughtfully. "Definitely chewing."

"Me, too."

She would have called it a night right then, but she didn't have the heart. Ron looked so happy. And in the grand scheme of things, what was one night of her life? Sighing, she asked if he was a Bazooka or Juicy Fruit man. Another half hour passed. Crabnutt talked about Teaberry, curling, and then worked his way right back to Phillips cross slot screwdrivers. Not once did he ask Gemma what she did for a living or inquire what her hobbies were. Finally Gemma stifled a yawn. "It's getting late. I really should be going." She rose from the table.

Ron followed suit. "This was really fun," he confessed shyly. Gemma's heart went out to him. He was boring, but still. Uncomfortable, she peered down at her feet.

"Can I call you?"

Gemma lifted her head and saw Ron nervously pull at his collar. "Sure," she returned softly, completely against her better judgment. She couldn't stand the thought of hurting him. Besides, how many guys actually called after taking your number? She gave it to him.

Fastening the front of her cape, she was careful to lift the back of her hair out from under it. Ron paid the bill, and together they walked outside, where Gemma hailed a cab.

"Talk to you soon," Ron said cheerily as he closed the door of the cab for her.

Once inside, Gemma was glad the turbaned cabbie was blasting the Jets game on the FAN. She'd had enough conversation for one evening.

Early the next morning, Gemma went to meet her closest friend, Francis "Frankie" Hoffmann, for breakfast. New Yorkers knew Frankie as "Lady Midnight," a deejay whose sexy, deep-throated voice filled the airwaves between midnight and 6 A.M. every Monday through Friday on WROX, the city's top-rated classic rock station. Gemma often met Frankie for an early-morning cup of coffee. Afterward, Gemma would head to her store in the Village, and Frankie would go home to crash.

Their favorite meeting place was the Happy Fork Diner on Thirty-fourth and Eighth, a twenty-four-hour greasy spoon run by two burly Greek brothers. Pushing through the heavy glass door, Gemma was greeted by the familiar smell of fresh coffee brewing. Sliding onto a booth's narrow Naugahyde bench, she waited for Stavros to take her order.

"Ah, Miss Gemma." Despite girth a pro wrestler might envy, Stavros always appeared out of nowhere, the steaming coffeepot in his gigantic, hairy hand dangerously full. "One taste. C'mon. One sip and you will never want to drink that peeswater tea again."

Gemma clucked with mock disapproval. "You know I don't do caffeine, Stavros."

"So?" He jutted his chin out. "I bring you decaf. Best decaf in New York."

Gemma batted her eyes at him, enjoying their little ritual. "Chamomile tea will be fine, thank you."

"Bah," he muttered, turning from the table. "An old lady's drink."

He's right, it is an old lady drink.

Stavros returned with her tea, muttering under his breath in Greek as he served her. Just then Frankie pushed through the door of the diner. On the air, Frankie sounded like a wet dream, her low, husky radio voice and teasing, kittenish laugh the perfect vocal accompaniment for the overnight hours. All the male listeners who called during her air shift begging for a date assumed she was a major babe. In truth, she was tall and painfully thin, with wispy blond hair she had a hard time styling and a spray of freckles across the bridge of her tiny stub nose.

"Sorry I'm late," Frankie said in her real voice, pure Brooklynese. She slipped into the booth opposite Gemma. "The Rock showed up late." The Rock, whose real name was Marshall Finklestein, was the jock on the air right after Frankie. He had a chronic problem telling the big hand from the little one.

Gemma squeezed her steeping tea bag before tipping a smidgen of soy milk into her mug. "I listened a bit between two and three. You sounded good."

"I screwed up the lead-in to 'Layla,' but oh well. Win some, lose some." Her gaze turned quizzical as Gemma's words sank in. "What were you doing up between two and three?"

"Not sleeping."

"Because—?"

"This and that." She proceeded to tell Frankie all about her riveting evening with her blind date, Big Red. Frankie kept a straight face as long as she could. But when Gemma got to the part where Crabnutt expounded on the virtues of chewing gum as opposed to collecting it, she lost it. She burst out laughing, and so did Gemma. There were tears rolling down their faces by the time Gemma was done.

"Oh, Lordy," said Frankie, swiping at her eyes. "I needed that."

"So did I."

"So, why the insomnia?" Frankie still wanted to know.

"I don't know." Gemma looked genuinely baffled. "I guess the date just got me thinking. Suppose I never find anyone?"

"I'm insulted you would even think that."

Gemma laughed. When she and Frankie were teenagers, they'd vowed that if they were both alone when they were old, they'd move in together. They'd rent male strippers, sunbathe nude, and ride motorcycles.

"You know what I mean."

"You're not going to be alone forever," Frankie consoled.

The sympathetic tone acted as a tonic to Gemma. It always did. She and Frankie were as close as sisters. Then Frankie took a deep breath and said, "Okay, let me ask you something." Gemma stiffened. "Okay, let me ask you something" was Frankie's standard windup to hitting Gemma between the eyes with the brutal truth.

"What?"

"Can't you cast a love spell for yourself?"

Gemma squirmed uncomfortably in her seat. Of course she could. But to her, witchcraft was a path centered around the reverence for nature she'd carried deep within her since she was a child. It was not about trying to bend nature to your will.

"Well?" Frankie prodded.

"I suppose I could."

"What's the point of being a witch if you don't use it to help yourself?"

"Maybe I'll do a spell tonight."

"Can I watch?"

"Sure. As long as you don't interrupt."

"I won't, I swear!" The look of excitement in Frankie's eyes faded, replaced by one of unmistakable distraction.

"What's wrong?"

"Nothing," Frankie murmured dismissively.

"Tell me."

"I've been feeling kind of confused lately. Plus, I have this." She pushed up her shirt sleeve, revealing a blister on her left forearm.

"So?"

"Necrotizing fasciitis. Flesh-eating disease. I have it, Gemma."

Gemma sighed deeply. To say Frankie was a hypochondriac was an understatement. Over the past year alone, Frankie had diagnosed herself with a brain tumor, West Nile virus, Crohn's disease, and a host of other ailments, all of which mysteriously faded in their own in time. Gemma rued the day she'd bought Frankie *The Merck Manual* as a joke.

"You do not have flesh-eating disease," Gemma said patiently.

"Oh, no? Two of the symptoms are mental confusion and blisters, both of which I have!"

"Are you sure you didn't burn your arm taking something out of the oven?"

"I'm sure."

"Then call up Dr. Bollard and make an appointment."

"I'm going to."

Gemma knew Frankie wouldn't call. She never did. Instead, she'd walk around convinced she had flesh-eating disease—until new symptoms appeared and then she'd move on to her next self-diagnosed ailment.

Frankie leaned toward Gemma eagerly. "So, do I get to be your assistant tonight? Hand you your eye of newt or whatever?"

"I'm a witch, not a magician! I don't need an assistant. All I need from you," she added under her breath just as Stavros approached to take their breakfast order, "is to send positive thoughts my way while I work the spell. Think you can do that?"

"If you promise to make me black bean tostadas for dinner."

Gemma extended a hand across the table for a shake. "Done."

Gemma got home from work itching to cast her spell.

"Just let me get changed," she told Frankie, who'd been waiting for her in the lobby of her building, eager to begin.

Frankie nodded, following Gemma into her bedroom as she changed into sweats.

"I still can't believe how gorgeous this place is," Frankie marveled.

"I know." Gemma loved this apartment now just as much as she did the day she moved in. Rather than selling, her cousin Michael's wife Theresa decided to rent her beautiful two-bedroom apartment on the Upper East Side. It had shining parquet floors, high ceilings, and a wall of windows looking out on the Fifty-ninth Street Bridge. It was by far the best place Gemma had ever lived in.

"Now what?" Frankie asked excitedly as Gemma headed back out to the living room.

"Follow me."

She led Frankie into the spare room, which had built in floor-to-ceiling bookcases lining three walls that Gemma had already filled to overflowing. French doors led out to a small terrace where she grew her herbs. In the center of the room were three standing candelabrums, each with four tapers, and a low round table draped in purple velvet cloth. The table held a small vase of fresh flowers and an old cracked pentacle. To the left of the vase were a gold candle, a ritual knife, a censer for incense, and a bowl of salt. To the right were a white candle, a silver chalice, and a bowl of water. A small silver plate held a few pins, matches, and various cones of incense.

"Now what?" Frankie asked again, eyes fixed on Gemma's altar.

"I'm going to light the candles. You sit over there." She pointed to one of two meditation cushions on the floor. Were she alone, she would probably cast a more elaborate, intense spell. But since Frankie had the attention span of a three-year-old on Christmas morning, she decided some simple candle magick would suffice.

Frankie did as she was told, slipping off her shoes before twisting her gangly legs into a modified pretzel position. Gemma lit the standing tapers. The room blazed to life around them.

"Now what?" Frankie whispered.

"Now you stop asking, 'Now what?'" Gemma whispered back, amused. She settled down on her meditation cushion opposite Frankie, large red candle in hand. She lit it, placing it on the floor before her. Closing her eyes, she struggled to concentrate. The sound of snarled traffic drifted up to her ears, but she blocked it out. She waited until she felt absolutely centered before opening her eyes and speaking softly.

"Okay, here's what we're going to do. We're both going to stare into the flame of that candle. In my mind, I'm going to think about the man I want to be with. You can do the same if you want."

Frankie wrinkled her nose. "Think about the man I want to be with, or the man you want to be with?"

"Either."

"Can it be someone famous? Like Russell Crowe?"

"It can be anyone. Russell Crowe. Russell Stover. Just concentrate."

"Okay." Brows furrowed, Frankie stared hard into the candle while Gemma did the same.

Describe the man you want to be with, Gemma.

It took a few seconds, but then the words came to her: I want someone confident, smart, honest, hardworking, and strong. Someone who loves nature the way I do. Someone loyal and sensitive, who'll respect who I am and what I do. Someone who'll love me just as I am.

She poured herself into these thoughts until she ran out of words to describe her dream man. The next step was to picture him.

"Picture him," she whispered to Frankie.

"Who?" Frankie whispered back.

"Russell Stover," Gemma replied impatiently.

This was harder. In her mind's eye, Gemma saw the hazy outline of someone tall, but when she tried to fill in the details of his face, she couldn't. The only thing she saw were his eyes. They were green . . . no, blue. Blue and wise and full of compassion. She still couldn't see his face, but now she could hear his laugh—deep, hearty—and delight swept through her. She wanted someone who laughed often. Someone unafraid to feel.

"Gemma?"

"Mmm?"

"I keep trying to picture Russell Crowe, but the only man who keeps coming to mind is Damian."

Gemma shuddered. Damian was Frankie's ex-husband. "Concentrate harder."

"I can't," Frankie said helplessly.

"Then concentrate on someone for me."

"Okay."

They sat a few minutes more in silence. Gemma kept trying to picture more details of her dream man, but none were forthcoming. She glanced at Frankie hopefully.

"See anything?"

"I see . . . I see . . . a big, steaming tostada on a plate."

Gemma sighed.

"What about you?" Frankie wanted to know. "Anyone?"

"Someone tall, with kind blue eyes and a really good laugh."

"Sounds promising."

Gemma reached forward and gently snuffed out the red candle.

Frankie looked disappointed. "That's it? No incantations? No flying monkeys? Nothing?"

"Feel free to say an incantation if you want."

"That's your realm, Glinda, not mine."

"Then I guess the spell is complete." Gemma hugged her knees to her chest. "Let's just hope it worked."

CHAPTER

02

Riding her bike to work the next morning, Gemma was upbeat. With any luck, Mr. Right could walk into her life today.

Her friends and family thought she was nuts to bike in the city, but for Gemma, nothing could beat watching the world pull past as she pedaled along, cutting her own, slow swath through the breeze. It was magic to be in motion, especially now that summer's stifling humidity was finally beginning to fade into fall. Her attention was drawn to every attractive man she pedaled past—could the cute guy in the weathered bomber jacket be the future father of her children? What about that sandy-haired fellow with the cell phone glued to his ear? Maybe he had gorgeous blue eyes . . .

Man watching made her reckless: Twice she nearly crashed into parked cars.

Arriving at her store, she whipped off her helmet, shaking out her hair before unlocking the door and carefully wheeling her bike to the small storage room in the back.

She had just lit a cone of juniper tree incense and put on a Brigit's Kiss CD when the front door bell tinkled. Anticipation shot through her. Smoothing the front of her long, peasant skirt, Gemma perched as delicately as she could on the stool behind the counter, anxiously hoping she'd catch sight of her dream man.

"Hi."

The man standing before her was pale and weedy. His sunken chest was lost inside a wrinkled black T-shirt with BLESSED BE in large white letters across the front. Hanging limply from his chin was a long, straggling blond beard. Yes, he had blue eyes—but they were the color of washed-out denim, not a Caribbean ocean. Gemma's heart sank. Sometimes, what you wanted and what the universe decided to send you were two very different things. Still, she managed to come up with a smile. "Hello. May I help you?"

The man reached into his pocket, handing her a crumpled newspaper clipping. It was the ad she'd placed in the *Village Voice* offering tarot classes. It was a way to help offset the costs of her ever-spiraling store rent.

"You're interested in learning tarot?"

The man nodded.

"What's your name?"

"Uther."

Gemma bit her lip. In her opinion, telling strangers your name was Uther or Gwyddion or Raven only gave the public more ammunition for not taking witchcraft seriously. She knew it was a person's right to use their Craft name publicly, but *still*.

"Uther what?" she prompted.

"Abramowitz."

"Uther Abramowitz," Gemma repeated thoughtfully. Was it possible the universe had sent her someone named Uther Abramowitz to love? If so, she was going straight home and dismantling her altar. She extended a polite hand across the counter. "I'm Gemma Dante."

Uther's grasp was limp, like a wet sock. The urge to bundle him up and hustle him to the deli for some minestrone soup was strong. "What do you do?" Gemma prodded.

"I write computer code."

Gemma smiled. Lots of Pagans held high-tech jobs. She wasn't sure why. "Well," she said, sliding off her stool, "let me explain how I work. I give private lessons. I also give a group lesson on Thursday nights—"

"I'd prefer private," Uther cut in immediately.

"Okay." Gemma pulled out her Palm Pilot from beneath the counter. "I have an opening at eight o'clock on Tuesday nights. Does that work for you?"

Uther shook his head. "Not really. Can you do any during the day? When the curtain of night falls, I'm pretty busy."

Doing what? Gemma wondered. *Watching* Lord of the Rings *for the 500th time?* Actually, she didn't want to know. "Well, if you'd be willing to come in during your lunch hour, say between noon and one, I could squeeze you in on Tuesdays."

"At your humble abode?" he asked eagerly.

"No, here in the store." Gemma fought to ignore the overt way he was checking her out. Did she really want to be alone with this odd duck for an hour every week? As subtly as she could, she read his aura, something she'd been able to do ever since she was a child. It was gray. He was confused, not evil. She could handle that.

"I charge sixty dollars an hour."

"'Tis a fair fee," Uther replied.

"I should have told you seventy-five," Gemma joked, hoping to pierce his solemn demeanor. But Uther just blinked. "That was a joke," Gemma clarified.

"Oh," said Uther.

"You'll need your own Rider-Waite deck," she continued. "If you don't already have one, you can buy one here."

"I don't have one," he mumbled, shoving his hands deep in his pockets.

Slipping out from behind the counter, Gemma led him to the locked glass case where she kept the tarot cards. Some, like those she'd recommended to him, were very basic and reasonably priced. But she also carried unique, more expensive decks, like the Dali Universal Tarot as well as one set of the much-sought-after, now-out-of-print Shakespearean Tarot.

"What deck do you use?" Uther asked shyly.

"Rider-Waite." Gemma pulled out a set for him that came with an accompanying booklet. "I still use the set I bought when I was twelve."

"How old are you now?" he blurted.

Gemma felt a blush go up to the roots of her hair. "That, kind sir, is classified information." Cards in hand, she walked back to the counter to ring them up. Strange as he was, there was something about Uther's utter lack of social skills that touched her.

"You don't need to buy any books right now," she noted. "The book that comes with the set is pretty good. Plus, I use handouts. But a lot of people like to put their cards in a box or bag to protect them from negative energy when they're not in use." She pulled out her own cards, which she kept in a small, purple velvet bag. "Would you like to buy a bag?"

Uther cleared his throat nervously. "Not now."

"That's fine," Gemma assured him, ringing up his order. "That comes to twenty-one sixty-five."

Pulling out two twenties, he guided them shyly into her palm. Making change, Gemma continued, "What I'd like you to do before next week is get used to handling the cards. Spend a few minutes each day shuffling them, touching them, and laying them out. Look at the images. See if any trigger images or visions. Go wherever your mind leads you. It may feel strange at first, but what you're doing is enlivening your imagination and building a rapport with the cards."

"What if I have to miss a class?" Uther asked.

Gemma handed him one of her business cards she kept in a seashell beside the cash register. "Just call and leave a message here at the store." She smiled as she passed him his purchase in a plain white bag. "Anything else?"

Uther shook his head no.

"See you next Tuesday, then," Gemma concluded brightly.

Uther dipped his head shyly. "Many thanks," he said, holding the bag aloft. "I'll make sure to do my homework."

"Don't think of it that way," Gemma urged. "Think of it as fun."

"Fun," he repeated to himself as if the concept were foreign. Looking befuddled, Uther Abramowitz made his way out of the store.

Gemma watched him leave. *What if . . . ?*

She couldn't bear to finish the thought.

PLEASE STOP STINKING UP THE BUILDING.

After a hard day at work, Gemma longed to meditate before dinner, but last week, someone had slipped a note under her door. Taking a box of matches from the mantelpiece, she hesitated before lighting her favorite Indian incense. It was probably Mrs. Croppy, the old woman across the hall, who had written it. She lived to make other tenants' lives miserable. Gemma lit the incense. If Mrs. Croppy had something to say, she should say it face-to-face.

The incense and a few well-placed candles created instant serenity. Dragging one of her meditation cushions out to the center of the living room, Gemma sat down in full lotus position. Eyes closed, breathing slowly, her body felt almost weightless as she floated in a dreamy, fragrant white cloud. She was calm. She was well.

Until someone started pounding fiercely on her door.

"Fire department!" a voice shouted. "If anyone's in there, open up!"

Fire department?

Gemma unfolded her legs and headed quickly to the front door. Peering through the spy hole, she saw three New York City firefighters staring back at her. Dressed in full firefighting regalia, each was holding a tool that looked like it could pry her door off its hinges in three seconds flat.

She fumbled to open the door. "Can I help you?"

"Evening, ma'am," said a firefighter with the bluest eyes Gemma had ever seen. "We received a report of smoke coming from your apartment."

Peering past the handsome firefighter, Gemma saw the door to the apartment directly across the hall open a crack, then abruptly shut. *Mrs. Croppy.*

Gemma smiled politely. "I'm sorry, but there's been a mistake."

But Blue Eyes wasn't listening. He was craning his neck to see into the apartment. He brushed past her, the other two firefighters following suit. Speechless, Gemma trailed them, then realized what pulled them in: ribbons of thick white smoke curling in the air and hanging like smog.

"Ma'am?" asked a short and stocky firefighter. He had a graying handlebar mustache that made him look turn-of-the-century.

"It's incense," Gemma explained. The third firefighter, exotic as an Aztec with huge black eyes and smooth caramel skin, began coughing violently.

"Jesus H. Christ," he wheezed. "It smells like a funeral parlor in here."

"It's incense," Gemma repeated.

"Yeah, well, it stinks," Mustache said harshly.

"It's supposed to."

Aztec looked dubious.

Meanwhile, Blue Eyes—who, Gemma noticed, had the word BIRDMAN painted in bright yellow on the back of his heavy black rubber jacket—snuffed out the joss sticks.

Gemma couldn't believe his lack of manners. "Do you mind?"

"Do *I* mind?" Blue Eyes echoed, incredulity in his voice. "Excuse me a moment." He got on his two-way radio, announcing the call was a false alarm. Hearing those two words, Gemma felt terrible. His expression was serious as he turned his attention back to her.

"I can see it's incense, but your neighbors had no way of knowing that. They were right to call the fire department, especially if this stuff was seeping out under the doorway."

"It wasn't," Gemma insisted lamely. *Was it?*

Blue Eyes folded his arms across his chest. "Then why are we here?"

Gemma studied the floor.

"No offense, ma'am, but this incense is too strong." He removed his helmet. Thick, black curls sprang to life as those gorgeous eyes scoured the ceiling. Gemma felt a small flutter in the pit of her stomach. He was movie star handsome, with a strong jawline. And those eyes . . .

"Do you have a working smoke detector?"

Gemma turned pink. "I guess."

"You guess?"

She didn't want to tell him she'd deliberately removed the batteries from it precisely so she could burn this particular sweet, smoky incense. Blue Eyes was shaking his head. She caught the glance he exchanged with the other two firefighters and her blush deepened. *They think I'm a strange, eccentric idiot who burns repulsive, stinky incense and wastes the fire department's time.*

"Where is the smoke detector?" Blue Eyes asked.

"In the bedroom."

"Mind if we check it?"

"I take it that's a rhetorical question."

"Why, yes, ma'am, it is."

Gemma sighed her capitulation, and pointed the way then followed, praying she hadn't left the room in a mess. Blue Eyes flicked on the light switch inside the doorway. Her bed was indeed made; but one of her black silk teddies was flung against her carefully arranged pillows. It looked provocative, an invitation without words. She tried to ignore it as each of the firefighters' eyes darted to the item in question. Aztec sniggered audibly and Blue Eyes cracked "Nice jammies" under his breath, thinking she wouldn't hear.

"Thank you," Gemma said pointedly, and he looked distinctly uncomfortable. *Good,* Gemma thought. *That's what you get.*

Mustache unscrewed the top of the smoke detector. Gemma tensed, knowing what he would find.

"Ma'am?" he inquired politely, removing his helmet to scratch his head. Mustache was bald as a newborn. With the handlebar mustache, gleaming pate, and firefighter garb, he could moonlight as a member of the Village People. "There's no battery in this smoke detector."

Gemma feigned surprise. "Oh?"

"It's also older than God," Mustache continued. "You could use a new one."

"I'll get one first thing tomorrow."

Meanwhile, Blue Eyes's attention was drawn to the walls, decorated with photos of animals: whales, elephants, dolphins, and monkeys. Gemma caught his eyes darting to the picture of Michael and Theresa she kept on her dresser, along with other family photos. His gaze seemed to linger there before returning to the walls. He studied her wildlife photos quietly but seriously—so seriously that Aztec followed suit.

"You cut those out of *National Geographic*?" Aztec asked.

"No, I took them myself."

Blue Eyes's gaze locked on her. "Really?"

"Yes. I love animals. I like to vacation where there's wildlife."

"Interesting," Blue Eyes murmured.

Mustache rolled his eyes. "We done here, Marlin Perkins?"

Blue Eyes gave Mustache a scowl, and Gemma was glad not to be on the receiving end of it. His expression remained grave as he addressed her. "You realize if there'd been an actual fire in here, it could have been quite serious, ma'am?"

"Please. My name is Gemma." *When did I go from a "miss" to a "ma'am"?*

"Gemma," Blue Eyes repeated, trying it out. "Interesting name."

"Thank you." Gemma's smile was genuine.

"Please get some fresh batteries and a new detector," he continued. "If not for your own safety, then for the safety of others in the building."

"I will," she promised. "I'm sorry about this."

"You should be. This could have been quite serious."

But it wasn't, Gemma thought. Talk about beating a dead horse! Were they taught to do that? "Are we done here?" she asked.

Aztec nodded.

Turning off the light, Gemma led them back into her living room. Was there a protocol here? Was she supposed to offer them coffee or something, especially since this was a false alarm? Was she supposed to make a donation to the FDNY?

Blue Eyes turned to Gemma. "Would it be possible for you to burn a less smoky brand of incense, miss, um—"

"Dante," Gemma supplied.

"Dante," he echoed thoughtfully. "Could you do that? Please?"

"I suppose." She'd been using this brand of incense for years. Now, thanks to Mrs. Croppy, she was going to have to find something else.

"A less smoky brand wouldn't trip a smoke detector," Blue Eyes continued.

Gemma bit her lip. "What if I took the batteries out whenever I burned the incense?"

It was a bad question.

"Do you know how many people take the batteries out of detectors when they're cooking and forget to put them back?" Blue Eyes said wearily. "Look, just buy a new smoke detector, put the batteries in, and leave them there. In the meantime, try to find a less pungent brand of incense"—he sounded amused, which bugged Gemma—"burn it for a shorter period of time, and keep a window cracked. That should take care of the problem."

Then he smiled at her, his blue eyes so alive and full of life that Gemma thought, *Old soul, Good heart,* and goose bumps rose up on her arms. Ushering them to the front door, she apologized again for wasting their time.

"*Yo, Birdman, whaddaya* think? A wacko or what?"

Hanging up his turnout coat back at the station, Sean Kennealy turned to answer the question posed to him by Sal Ojeda, who, along with Mike Leary, had just helped him perpetrate a minor fraud on his neighbor.

"Could be." Sean shrugged. "I just hope she stops burning that crap."

"Oh, she will," Leary predicted, sliding out of his boots. "You were very professional."

Sean chuckled. For over a month, the smell coming out of Theresa Falconetti's old apartment had been driving him crazy. He'd come home from his shift, desperate for sleep, but he couldn't. The stinky smell wafting its way to his apartment was so strong it was suffocating. Opening all of his windows didn't help. The stink clung to the air, tormenting him. One morning, sleep deprived and pissed off, he slipped a note under the apartment's door, hoping that would do the trick.

Then two nights later the stench returned.

That bugged him.

Years earlier, someone down the hall had complained that Pete and Roger squawked their heads off whenever he wasn't home. He'd tracked down a vet who was able to prescribe some antianxiety meds. Presto! Problem solved. If he could respond to a neighbor's request, why couldn't the incense burner? Was his note too nasty? True, he'd scribbled it in haste. Maybe he should have knocked on the door and asked The Stinker to stop? But he was in no mood to get into it with someone who might be a wacko. What kind of person *wants* their apartment to smell like that?

Instead, Sean asked two of his buddies from the firehouse to help him take care of the problem once and for all. They waited until their shift was over, then bunkered up and walked over to his building on Fifty-ninth and First, feeling like three naughty schoolboys. Seeing where he lived, Leary and Ojeda razzed him about being Yuppie scum, but Sean offered no apologies. Years back, he'd worked hard on Wall Street to buy his apartment. Now he owned it outright and was proud of it.

"You catch that teddy on the bed?" Leary drawled. "I bet she was waiting for her guru to come over and take her to a higher plane, if you know what I mean."

Ojeda laughed. "All the way to nirvana, baby."

Sean laughed, too. He had expected The Stinker to be

some kind of urban ascetic, gaunt and unsmiling. Instead, the door was opened by a tiny, curvaceous woman with wild, tumbling red hair and the kindest eyes he had ever seen. Her poise impressed him; so had the photos on her bedroom walls. Leary's "Marlin Perkins" crack had annoyed him, because it kept him from finding out more about Gemma Dante, who was obviously related to the hockey player, Michael Dante, Theresa's husband. The photo on the dresser was a dead giveaway. Was Gemma his sister?

On the other hand, Leary's ribbing was a good thing. Yeah, they rode him hard about being "Birdman," but teasing the shit out of the guys at the house was a firefighter's favorite pastime. Since he'd come from Wall Street, it had taken them a long time to accept him. The wisecracks meant he was one of them.

Down the hall, the current shift at Engine 31/Ladder 29 was sitting down to dinner. Sean could smell the enticing aroma of Al Dugan's famous "Help! My butt's on fire!" chili as it wafted onto the apparatus floor, making his stomach rumble.

"You guys up for a burger and a beer?" he asked.

"Depends," Ojeda said. "You paying?"

"What, in return for services rendered?"

"Shit, you make us sound like hookers," Leary said. He turned to Ojeda. "Don't make the man pay for a favor, you cheap little bastard."

"What?" Ojeda whined. "It's burgers and beers, for Chrissakes, not filet mignon and Dom."

Leary thought a moment then turned back to Sean. "The little bastard's got a point."

Sean grinned. "Geez, if I'd known you two were such cheap dates, I'd have asked you out sooner. Shall we?"

Together, the three men left the firehouse and headed down the street.

•　　　•　　　•

The first thing Gemma did when she saw her cousin Michael in the green room at Met Gar the next night was playfully punch him in the arm.

"Ouch!" Michael recoiled, rubbing the spot where her fist had landed. "What was *that* for?"

"That blind date you set me up on! All he talked about was screwdrivers and *gum!*"

"He's a nice guy!" Michael retorted.

"There's a difference between nice and boring."

Michael shrugged philosophically. "So it didn't work out. What matters is you did a nice thing, right?"

"True."

"C'mere, give cousin Mikey a hug, you do-gooder, you."

Gemma stepped into her cousin's embrace. It always amazed her how solid he felt. He'd been a scrawny little thing when they were kids, all pointy elbows and knobby knees and lack of coordination. And now look at him, Gemma marveled. Mr. NHL Bigshot.

And happily married, too, to the woman of his dreams, with a new baby girl. Pride burgeoned within Gemma as she recalled the pivotal role she'd played in getting Michael and Theresa together. It hadn't been easy; both were stubborn as mules, not to mention melodramatic. But with a little help from some tarot cards and a big, heaping dose of Dante family–style meddling, she'd helped them past their foolish pride and into each other's arms.

"So, who are you playing tonight?" she asked as they gently broke their embrace.

Utter disbelief flitted across Michael's face. "Do you ever bother to crack open a newspaper? Or are you too busy stirring your cauldron?"

"You're hilarious."

"I try."

"Seriously, Michael, who are you playing?" Gemma repeated, pushing back the hair from her forehead. Sometimes she just wanted to cut it all off, it was so wavy and unruly. "I've been really, really busy, I didn't have time—"

"Sshh." He put his index finger to her lips. "Relax. It's okay." Removing his hand, he said, "We're playing an exhibition game against the FDNY hockey team. The proceeds will benefit the Uniformed Firefighters Association Scholarship Fund. It's for kids whose dads got badly burned, or, you know . . ."

Died, Gemma supplied in her head. *Kids whose dads died.* Though it had been over four years since 9/11, it was still hard for New Yorkers to talk about it. Gemma nodded her understanding.

"I had a little adventure with the fire department myself," she said, trying to lighten the mood. She told Michael about the incense and the false alarm.

His response was typical. "Well, if it was the same stuff you burn in the store, I'm not surprised someone called the fire department. You could clear the block with that crap."

Gemma clucked her tongue. "You're an idiot, you know that?"

"Yeah, but you love me, anyway." His eyes shot to the clock on the wall. "I gotta go get dressed. You know where to sit, right?"

"Of course." Gemma glanced around the green room. She recognized some of the players there. The rest, she assumed, were members of the players' families, just like her. But why was she the only Dante present? "Theresa is coming, right?"

"Yeah, she's just running behind. She'll be here."

"And Anthony?"

Anthony was Michael's older brother, as well as the head chef and half owner of the family restaurant they owned in Brooklyn, Dante's. Hearing Gemma's question, Michael guffawed.

"Yeah, right. Like I could get him to leave his battle station at the stove on a Saturday night." He launched into an imitation of his brother. "'I run a business, Mikey. I can't just drop my freakin' ladle and run every time you shoot a puck down the friggin' ice for some *ubatz* charity.'"

The impersonation was so accurate Gemma erupted into appreciative laughter. "I guess that answers the question." Rising up on tiptoes, she gave Michael a kiss on the cheek. "I'm kind of beat, so I don't know if I'll see you after the game. But good luck."

"Thanks." He went to leave, then turned back, eyes gleaming with mischief. "Oh, and Gem?"

"Yeah?"

"We're the guys in blue and white with BLADES written on the front of our jerseys. Just so you know."

CHAPTER

03

Met Gar was packed. Gazing at the sea of exuberant faces as she took her seat behind the Blades' bench, Gemma noticed most of the people were families, many wearing T-shirts and baseball caps bearing the FDNY logo. Watching a father ruffle his young daughter's hair before rising to order a hot dog for each of them, Gemma ached with envy and longing. Though she adored her family, she was considered somewhat of a "black sheep." Her eyes continued surveying the buzzing crowd, her attention drawn to the many children there. How many were father-less? How many had lost cousins, uncles, sons, brothers? Like most New Yorkers, she'd pretty much taken firefight-ers and what they did for granted. That is, until over three hundred of them died trying to save others on a bright, clear morning in September. Ever since then, they'd been lauded as heroes and christened sex symbols. Gemma hadn't thought about them being sexy until Blue Eyes and his cohorts came pounding on her door.

Blue Eyes. Just picturing his handsome, rugged face

made her run hot and cold all over. She wondered if he was here to cheer his buddies on, and if so, if their paths might cross.

"There you are!"

At the sound of Theresa's voice, Gemma turned. Silly though it was, she was feeling semiconspicuous sitting there alone, wondering if the surrounding families thought she was a puck bunny. She certainly didn't dress like a hockey groupie; that much she knew for sure. Unless bunnies had taken to wearing chunky, silver earrings, flowing floral scarfs, and maroon velvet trousers.

"Hey, you." Theresa's smile was warm as she maneuvered herself into a seat. "Know how I knew you were already here?"

"How?"

Theresa lifted her nose in the air and sniffed. "Your perfume. Very distinctive."

Gemma chuckled. "Is that good or bad?"

"It's good. Kind of tangerine-y." Theresa took in the crowd. "*Madonn'*, the place is packed."

"They'll raise a lot of money."

"Hope so."

Reaching into her purse, Theresa took out a scrunchie and pulled her black, wavy hair into a loose ponytail. Gemma detected a few strands of gray in the mix; not that it mattered. If anything, it made the beautiful Theresa look even more exotic. Though she did look tired in that way many new mothers do.

"So, how's the baby?" Gemma wanted to know, squeezing Theresa's arm.

Theresa's smile was weary but happy. "Great."

"Have you named her yet?" Though their daughter was a month old, Theresa and Michael had yet to agree on a name. Michael wanted Philomena, after his mother. Theresa's reaction had been concise: "Over my dead body." Theresa was pushing hard for Galen. Michael said that sounded like an antacid.

"The way we're going, she's going to wind up being called 'Miss X.'"

Gemma smiled sympathetically. "Don't worry, you'll come up with something." Taking the jumbo-sized bottle of Evian from Theresa's hand, she helped herself to a sip. "I'm surprised you're here. I thought for sure you'd be home with Miss X."

"The first baby ever born in the history of the world is with my mother, God save her tiny, unnamed soul. No, I'm here because one of the Blades is a client and he's slated to do an interview after the game. I want to make sure he doesn't say anything stupid." She took the water back from Gemma. "And I wanted to support Michael, of course."

"Of course."

Gemma opened her mouth to say something else but was drowned out by the blaring horn signaling the game was about to begin. Since it was a charity game, they'd be playing only two periods. Though she enjoyed watching her cousin play, Gemma wasn't a big sports fan in general. She traced it back to elementary school phys ed, when she was always chosen last for basketball because of her height and teased unmercifully for her inability to hit a softball.

Since Met Gar was the Blades' home ice, they skated out first. A rousing cheer rose up from the crowd as each player skated out into the spotlight. Gemma noticed that Michael, especially, got a thundering reception, proof of his status as hometown favorite. He loved it, too, waving and smiling as he made a circuit round the ice before gliding to the players' bench.

"Your husband is such a ham," she remarked to Theresa, who heartily agreed.

As loud as the cheers were for the Blades, the decibel level went sky high when the FDNY hockey team appeared, their bright red jerseys dazzling against the white ice. Unlike the Blades, the players for the fire department hockey team came in all shapes and sizes. There were neckless little runts who would be pulverized by one modest hit from a Blades defenseman, refrigerator-sized brutes, and tall, sleek geeks Gemma could envision being blown over by the passing breeze created by a fast-skating teammate.

And there was Blue Eyes.

She turned to Theresa. "Do you have a program?"

"Sure."

Gemma eagerly flipped through the pages until she came to the FDNY players. There he was, Number 45, Sean Kennealy of Ladder 29 Company. Kennealy. Of course. Blue eyes, dark hair . . . he was "Black Irish."

Sean Kennealy. He was playing defense, probably because of his size. He was huge. Strapping. A strapping Irishman.

The puck dropped, and then both sides were in motion, one of the Blades carrying the puck, of course.

Since it was a charity game, the Blades weren't playing as hard or fast as usual. None of them really checked any of the firefighters, and the tempo of the skating was turned down a notch. That is, until the FDNY team scored a goal seven minutes in. After that, the Blades decided to be a little less kind.

None of it mattered to Gemma. Her eyes were glued to Sean Kennealy, whether he was on the ice or off it. She was no hockey expert, true, but he seemed fearless when he played, his expression as menacing as that of any NHL defensemen. Nor did he seem to shy from physical contact; unless Gemma was mistaken, he was one of the few FDNY players actually daring to fully check members of the Blades' offense. The game ended in a tie—"Rigged," Theresa whispered to Gemma—and people began the slow, shuffling departure from Met Gar.

"So," Theresa said to Gemma, "will I see you at Miss X's christening next weekend?"

"Of course." Gemma's eyes were still on the ice, picturing Sean as he confidently checked her own cousin.

Theresa leaned over to whisper in her ear. "Earth to Gemma, game's over."

Gemma turned to Theresa, smiling apologetically. "Sorry."

Filing out of the arena, she discreetly tucked the evening's program into her bag.

"I'm surprised the altar didn't burst into flames when you walked into church."

Ignoring her cousin Anthony's comment, Gemma rose up on tiptoes to plant an affectionate kiss on his cheek. They were standing among family and friends outside St. Finbar's Church in Bensonhurst, where Michael and Theresa had just had their infant daughter christened. Gemma had blanched when she'd heard the name they settled on: Domenica. Domenica Dante. It sounded like a deranged Italian film director. But she understood why they'd chosen it: They were honoring Theresa's father, Dominic, who had passed away two and a half years earlier.

Gemma's gaze ranged over the noisy group assembled on the church steps. She watched as her relatives jostled each other for their turn to have their picture snapped holding the baby, who was serene as a doll in her antique ivory gown. Gemma knew Anthony's wisecrack wasn't malicious, but it still smarted.

Happy tears had flooded Gemma's eyes during the ceremony. She'd watched Michael and Theresa lovingly convey their daughter from the front pew up to the baptismal font, accompanied by the godparents: Anthony, and Theresa's best friend, Janna. Gemma had been able to say hi to Janna and her husband Ty before the ceremony, but hadn't had a chance to chat with Anthony and his wife until now.

In fact . . .

"Where's Angie?"

Anthony frowned. "On duty. Couldn't get off. She's gonna try and swing by the party later."

The party was being held at Dante's a few blocks away. Once a neighborhood secret, it had become outrageously trendy. Anthony claimed he hated the Manhattanites who now descended regularly, but Gemma never heard him complain about all the money the restaurant was generating.

The baby, whom Gemma was aching to hold, had just been passed to cousin Paul, who had come in from Long Island with his wife and kids. Gemma started to move toward them—it had been months since she'd seen Paul and his family—but stopped dead in her tracks. Her mother, Aunt Betty Anne, and Aunt Millie were marching down the church steps heading straight for her. Anthony, rather than sentimentally noting that his late mother, the fourth Grimaldi sister, was missing, nudged Gemma in the ribs. "Heads up. Here come Mo, Larry, and Curly."

Gemma moved tentatively in the direction of her mother, who had pointedly ignored her in church. *Please don't make a scene, Mom.*

"Hello, Mom." Gemma leaned in to kiss her mother's cheek; her mother flinched slightly. She also kissed her aunts. Millie covertly winked at her as if to say, "Don't mind your mother," but Betty Anne was cold as marble.

"You look good," Aunt Millie croaked, her gravelly voice betraying her lifelong, three-pack-a-day Winston habit.

"I can't believe you came to church," her mother snapped.

"I was invited, Mom." Gemma was determined not to take the bait. "I'm a member of this family, too."

"You should have just come to the party. To show up at the house of God . . ." She made the sign of the cross while emitting a heavy theatrical sigh.

"Don't start," Gemma implored quietly.

"I'm not starting anything," her mother insisted shrilly, eyeing her younger sisters for backup. "Am I?"

Betty Anne's eyes fell to the ground. Millie excused herself for a smoke. That said it all. God forbid anyone stand up to Constance Annamaria Grimaldi Dante.

"I'm going to go talk to Nonna," Gemma informed her mother politely. *I tried,* she told herself. *That's what matters.*

Still, she felt like she'd been punched in the stomach.

She found her grandmother still inside the church, talking to one of the priests. Nonna's tiny, gnarled hands were waving madly, while the rapid-fire patter of her voice told Gemma that this priest was not number one in Nonna's hit parade. Gemma approached carefully, not wanting to interrupt. But the minute her grandmother caught sight of her, the tirade halted and she broke into a wide, delighted smile.

"*Bella,* I've been waiting for you!" She smiled knowingly at the young priest. "This is my granddaughter, Gemma. Bet you wish priests could get married, eh?"

"Nonna!" Gemma turned to the priest. "Please, Father. She didn't mean it."

The priest coughed uncomfortably and hurried off, clearly relieved to be free of speaking to an old devil like Nonna.

"I can't believe you did that!"

"What, told the truth?" Nonna snorted, watching the priest hustle up the center aisle of the church. "Tight ass," she added disdainfully.

"Nonna!" Gemma exclaimed again. Depending on who you asked, Maria Grimaldi was either "a pip," "a character," "a loon," or "a royal pain in the ass." To Gemma, she was simply Nonna, the grandmother she adored, and who loved her unconditionally.

"Here, let me look at you."

Gemma dutifully held still beneath her grandmother's loving eye, Nonna's head bobbing in approval. "Beautiful."

"You always say that."

"Because it's always true." Her hand clasped Gemma's forearm for support. Gemma jumped.

"Nonna, your hands are freezing!"

"My blood's getting too tired to make the full round." She waved a hand in the air. "It happens."

That was Nonna: no nonsense, philosophical about the passing of time. She'd been a great beauty, and to Gemma was beautiful still, with her long, white braid and her big, green eyes that were always alert, always watchful. "Have you held the bambina yet?" Nonna asked.

"Not yet. There's quite a crowd around her."

"She's gorgeous. Perfect. Her name is Theresa."

"Theresa is her mother, Nonna," Gemma laughed. "The baby is Domenica."

"Right, right," Nonna replied hastily. "Domenica." Slowly, they made their way toward the open church doors to join the rest of the family.

"So, your mother," Nonna began, her steps small and careful.

Gemma's eyes darted down to meet her grandmother's. "What about her?"

"Is she still upset about *La Stregheria,* or—?"

"Still upset."

"She needs a swift kick in the ass, that one."

Gemma chuckled. "A swift kick in the ass" was one of her grandmother's favorite expressions. It was actually made endearing by the soft edges of her Italian accent, which had worn away over the years.

"There's more than one way to worship, *cara.*"

"I agree with you there."

She gave Gemma's arm a squeeze. "You and me, we're a lot alike. Now, how about you give me a ride over to the restaurant?"

Nonna had the knack of turning a simple ten-minute jaunt into an hour-long production.

First, they had to stop by the house of Mrs. Crochetti, one of the women in Nonna's prayer circle, so Nonna could check up on her. Apparently, Mrs. Crochetti was suffering with a goiter. Next, Nonna had to be driven to the bakery to pick up bread, since it would be closed by the time the christening party was over. Finally, they had to go to Nonna's house to drop off the bread and pick up baby Domenica's christening gift, which required wrapping. By the time Gemma's battered old Beetle rattled into the restaurant parking lot, they were forty minutes late and the party was in full swing.

Gemma guided Nonna through the door, where they were bombarded by the sound of happy conversation among friends and relatives. The place was packed. Some people were already seated; others stood in small groups with drinks in hand, talking. It seemed more like a wedding reception than a baptismal bash for a tiny baby. Then again, Theresa was a publicist and Michael was the New York Blades' hometown hero. No wonder the room was packed.

"Who do you want to sit with?" Gemma asked her grandmother.

Nonna took her time assessing the crowd, finally pointing to a small, round table near the kitchen doors where Gemma's mother and her two sisters sat.

Gemma peered at her grandmother. "You sure? You might have more fun if you sat with someone else. Mussolini, for instance."

Nonna chuckled. "What could be more fun than making my daughters hot under the collar?"

"Well, don't come crying to me when Mom cuts you off after one glass of grappa."

As carefully as she could, Gemma maneuvered her grandmother through the dense, upbeat crowd. The baby was nowhere in sight. Theresa had probably taken her off somewhere to nurse. Seeing Gemma and Nonna approach the table, Gemma's mother frowned.

"We only have room for one here, and we're savin' this seat for Robert DeNiro."

Aunt Betty Anne gasped. "Bobby D is *here?*"

"Bobby D!" Aunt Millie snorted. "Like you know him!"

Betty Anne looked insulted. "We *do* go to the same podiatrist," she sniffed. "Bunions," she added knowingly.

"He's a client of Theresa's," Gemma's mother said. "He could come. You never know."

"He can go sit with Al Pacino, then," Gemma said as she helped Nonna into the empty seat.

"There goes our fun," Gemma mother's grumbled.

"Take a pill, will ya?" Aunt Millie snapped, lighting up. She squeezed Gemma's hand.

"Thanks for bringing her over here, doll. We'll make sure she stays out of trouble." She craned her neck, anxiously looking around the room. "I don't see Al Pacino."

Content her grandmother was now settled, Gemma headed for the bar. If anyone deserved a drink right now, it was her. That's when she saw him. Blue Eyes, Sean Kennealy, firefighter/hockey player in all his heart-stopping glory. He was holding a pint of beer and talking to Michael like they were old friends.

What was he doing here?

She made her way toward him, hoping she wouldn't face another lecture on fire safety. Michael's timing couldn't have been better: He moved off to speak with another cluster of guests just as Sean scoured the crowd and happened to light on Gemma. Seeing the smile on his face as their eyes met, Gemma felt a joyful heat surging through her body, radiant and strong.

"Hi," she said shyly, reaching his side.

"Hey." He seemed genuinely pleased to see her. "Gemma Dante, right?"

She nodded. "You have a good memory."

"It's not an easy name to forget." He squinted slightly, studying her face. "Are you Michael's sister?"

"No, we're double cousins." Seeing his puzzled expression, she added, "Our fathers were brothers and our mothers were sisters." Then she changed the subject. "How do you know Michael?"

"Through, uh, the FDNY hockey team."

"I was at the game the other night. The charity game."

Sean looked curious. "So, what did you think?"

"I think it was fixed."

Sean chuckled appreciatively. "The Blades probably could have played a little harder, you're right." He took a quick sip of beer. Gemma watched the bob of his Adam's apple as he swallowed and thought it the sexiest thing in the world. "But it's all for a good cause."

"I agree."

"Can I get you a drink?"

"That would be great."

"What's your pleasure?"

Better not answer that, she thought. "A gin and tonic would be great."

He smiled then, and it was killer. "Be back in a minute."

She watched as he made his way to the bar. God, he was a looker. And his body—muscled thighs evident through his faded jeans, strong shoulders swathed in a blue-and-white-striped oxford shirt, sleeves casually rolled. *No wedding ring.*

Taking her drink from him, she took a small sip, grateful for something to do with her hands. "Are you ever going to tell me your name, 'Birdman'?" She knew, of course, but she wanted to hear him say it, wanted to hear his deep, sexy voice caress the syllables.

He ducked his head shyly. "It's Sean. Sean Kennealy."

"Irish?"

"Just a bit." He took a long pull off his beer, his eyes seeming to dance with mischief. "So, have you gotten a new smoke detector yet, Gemma?"

Gemma colored. "Not yet. But I'm going to, I swear."

"Maybe I'll buy you one. As a present," he teased.

"If that's your idea of a present a woman would enjoy, then I pity you." They both laughed. "What does 'Birdman' mean?"

He looked uncomfortable. Gemma hoped she hadn't just put her foot in it. Suppose it had to do with sex? She braced herself.

"It's my nickname at the firehouse. I rescued these two birds from a fire and wound up adopting them. Ever since then, they've called me 'Birdman.'"

"Are nicknames big with firemen?"

"Huge. But not all of them can be repeated in mixed company. And since you're clearly a lady, I'll spare you."

For some reason, his calling her "a lady" sent giddiness charging through Gemma. *Is he aware of how sexy he is?* Two big gulps of gin and tonic slid down her throat.

"I loved those photos in your bedroom," he continued. "Are you a professional photographer?"

"Only in my dreams. In real life I run a boutique in the Village called the Golden Bough."

His brow furrowed. "Interesting."

"Is it?"

"Yeah. I don't run into too many businesswomen in my line of work. Unless their business has burned down."

"What kind of women do you run into? If you don't mind me asking."

"Not at all." He took another sip of beer. "Most of the guys' wives and girlfriends are regular working people:

schoolteachers, housewives, nurses—nothing fancy like owning their own business." He winked at her.

"It's not fancy. It's just what I always wanted to do."

He raised his glass to her. "I hear you."

"You too? You always wanted to be a firefighter?"

"Hell, no. I fought that for years! I've only been with the department for three years. Before that, I was a stock-broker." He put his index finger to his lips. "Don't tell any-one. People hear that and all of a sudden they treat me like I'm Merrill Lynch."

Gemma laughed. "I promise, I will never ask you for fi-nancial advice."

Sean's eyes caressed her body. "You don't look like you need it."

Gemma blushed, the bold compliment catching her off guard. She scrambled to keep the conversation going. "What made you switch careers?"

"Destiny. My dad was a ladder man and my granddad was an engine man. You can't outrun what's in the blood, you know?"

"But wasn't it hard? I mean, you must have gone from making a tremendous amount of money to—" Her hand flew to her mouth. "I'm sorry. That's none of my business."

"No, it's okay." Sean patted her shoulder reassuringly. "I like the fact you say what most people think. And the answer is yes, I took a big cut in salary. But the money's not why we do it." He eyed her curiously. "Enough about me. I want to hear about your store. Where is it?"

"In the Village. Thompson Street."

"I don't know the Village that well," he confessed.

"Oh." Gemma was surprised. "Don't you live in New York?"

"Yeah," he said evasively. "But I'm from Long Beach, originally."

"New Jersey?"

"Long Island."

Gemma nodded. She'd heard of Long Beach, but had never been there. Her only experience with Long Island was with her cousin Paulie's house in Commack.

"One of the guys at 35 Engine has an apartment right on the boardwalk," Sean continued. "Sometimes we switch apartments for the weekend, especially in the winter. He gets to play in the city, and I get to wake up to the sound of the ocean for a few days."

Gemma could picture it: the insistent cries of the gulls coasting on invisible currents of wind; the soothing rhythm of the tides; the sun dancing playfully off the surface of the waves, creating a kaleidoscope of diamonds. It had to be wonderful in the spring and summer. But the winter? "Isn't it lonely in the winter?"

"Are you kidding? Winter is when the beach is best." His tone bordered on the rapturous. "There's no one there. It's glorious."

She asked more questions, and he answered them all, though she got the sense he didn't really like talking about himself. Still, she learned that he was from a big Irish family and that most of them lived on Long Island. He'd been playing hockey since he was small, and one of his brothers-in-law—also a firefighter—was trying to talk him into learning the bagpipes. Sean was reluctant. Hockey took up enough of his time; he didn't need another hobby. When it was time to sit down for dinner, she was thrilled when he asked to sit with her. He ordered veal, then must have seen the disappointment in her eyes.

"You don't eat meat?" he asked.

"My rule is to never eat anything with a face."

Sean shot her a look. "I'm not touching that one."

Dinner flew by. They talked about hockey, the beach, animals, and photography. After dessert Gemma excused herself to search for Domenica. Come hell or high water, she was going to cuddle that baby before the night was through. She found mother and child sitting on the battered old couch in the restaurant's business office.

"Someone needed her diaper changed," Theresa explained as Gemma came toward them. "And someone else needed a few moments of peace and quiet."

Gemma held out her arms. "Hand her over."

Theresa smiled proudly as she passed her daughter to Gemma.

"She's gorgeous." Gemma cradled the baby in her arms. Domenica's perfect, rosebud mouth was closed, but her big green eyes were wide open and curious, framed with the longest lashes Gemma had ever seen. "She's going to be a stunner."

"Don't let Michael hear that. He'll get on the Internet and order a chastity belt now." Both women laughed, and Theresa stifled a long yawn. "Sorry. I'm exhausted."

"You must be."

"Miss Thing here likes to sleep all day and stay awake all night."

"You should have named her Vampira."

"Can you suggest herbs or anything?" Theresa asked seriously.

"For you or for her?"

"Both. I'm tired, and she's gassy."

"She's a true Dante. Michael and Anthony used to have farting contests when they were small."

Theresa sucked in her cheeks, mildly appalled. "Thanks for sharing that, Gem."

"My pleasure. You should take ginseng for energy. As for Princess here"—she brushed her lips against the velvety soft perfection of Domenica's forehead, reveling in her gorgeous baby scent—"there's a tonic called Baby's Bliss Gripewater. You can find it in any good health food store. It's got fennel and ginger in it, which should relieve stomach pain."

Theresa looked grateful as her body slumped farther down the couch. "How can I ever repay you?"

Gemma's mouth turned up into a sly smile. "Tell me everything you can about Michael's adorable firefighter friend, Sean Kennealy."

Theresa snorted. "Michael's friend? I'm the one who invited Sean! I've known him for years."

Gemma blinked. "But he said he knew Mike through the fire department's hockey team."

"Well, maybe he does, but he knows me from the building. He's been living in the apartment above mine—now yours—for years." She looked baffled. "I thought for sure you guys already met. You've been chatting away all night like bosom buddies."

Gemma gingerly handed Domenica back to her mother and edged quietly toward the door. "Can you excuse me a minute? I just remembered something I was supposed to tell Anthony."

"Sure."

Leaving the office, Gemma's mind turned to Sean Kennealy. *That devil!* she thought, not without affection. Beginning to put two and two together, she went back out to join him at the party. Sean Kennealy didn't know it yet, but his feet were about to be put to the fire. Only this time, it wouldn't be in the line of duty.

CHAPTER

04

The Dante family reminded Sean of his own.

They were large, close knit, and obviously enjoyed each other's company. They also knew how to have a good time, if the free flow of wine and spontaneous bursts of song were any indication. But while any friction in his family was subterranean, with the Dantes it was right out in the open. Michael and Anthony were shouting at each other one minute, hugging the next. And despite pointing her out to him, Gemma hadn't spoken with her mother all evening.

Gemma. Gem-ma Dan-te.

Her name sounded musical to him. Lyrical. They'd spent almost the entire party together, and he was seriously attracted to her. She seemed gentle and sweet, a genuinely good person. A bit New Age-y—he was skeptical when she suggested some herb for the carbon monoxide headaches he got from eating smoke. Meditation, herbs, vegetarianism—they weren't his thing. He was a man who liked steak for dinner, aspirin for headaches, and when he wanted to relax, he read Alan Furst or watched the History Channel. But she was just trying to help. He liked how she looked, too. She was petite. *Five foot three,* he thought. *If that.* Yet she wasn't small. She had curves in the right places. Soft, that's what she was. Soft.

Best of all, she'd never dated a firefighter, wasn't related to a firefighter, and seemed to know nothing about firefighter culture. She was different, new, interesting. How that would go down with his buddies, he wasn't sure. He could already imagine the comments he'd get for dating a woman who probably made three times what he did. But that was putting the cart before the horse. First he had to get her to go out with him. And then . . . Sean drained his beer and ordered another. Just thinking about making love to her made him throb. That long red hair, those plump, curvy hips . . . God she was sexy.

"There you are."

A thrill shot through him as Gemma sidled up to him. He'd been sitting at the bar listening to her cousin Anthony, who was expounding on ricotta while puffing on a fat cigar.

"I thought smoking was banned in restaurants," Gemma said.

"Not when you own the place and it's a private party," Anthony declared.

Gemma shook her head. "It's bad for you, Ant."

"Listen to Miss Incense over here. All of a sudden she's the Surgeon frickin' General," he cracked to Sean. He snuffed out the offending stogie nonetheless. "There. Happy?"

"Very. And so are your lungs."

"*Madonn',* you're worse than Angie, I swear to God." He wiped his hands on his apron. "I'm being a bad host. Sean, this is my cousin Gemma. Gemma—"

"We've met." She smiled at Sean sweetly. "Sean and

two of his buddies tricked me into thinking someone had called the fire department to complain about my incense."

Sean spit up beer. "Excuse me," he rasped, turning away to cough into a napkin. *Damn. Busted.* He had planned to come clean with her at the end of the evening, preferably while they were alone, driving back to the city together.

"I don't understand," Anthony said thickly.

"It's a long story," Sean muttered.

Gemma's eyes flashed wickedly. "Shall I tell it?"

Sean used *his* eyes to plead for clemency. "I don't think that's necessary, do you?"

"I don't know. You sent the note, too, didn't you?"

Before Sean could answer, Anthony swung off the bar stool, his discomfort obvious. "Okeydokey. You guys are communicating in some bizarro code. I'm going to say *adios.*" He leaned down for a quick kiss to Gemma's cheek. "I'm going to take Nonna home now. She seemed a little off today, no?"

Gemma nodded absently, amused eyes still fixed on Sean.

"Too much vino, I bet," Anthony surmised, then walked away.

Alone with Gemma now, Sean launched his plea. "Look—"

"Confession time. Did you send the note?"

Sean's shoulders slumped. "Yes."

Gemma chuckled. "Why not just knock on my door and tell me face-to-face to stop burning incense? Why send a nasty note?"

Sean looked sheepish. "Because I had a killer headache and was in no mood to get into it with a stranger. Besides, that sh—incense you burn is strong. Admit it."

"What's wrong with strong?"

"Nothing, if the smell is nice. Like your perfume, for example."

She blushed, and he knew he was home free. Or so he thought.

"You said you knew Michael from the FDNY hockey team."

"I do know Michael through the hockey team!"

"That's splitting hairs. You purposely didn't tell me you knew Theresa from the building."

"You're right. I'm sorry." Feeling bold, he let his knuckles brush her cheek. "Anything I can do to make it up to you?"

He could see from the red rushing once again into her face that she was thinking the same thing he was.

Gemma suddenly seemed to turn shy. "Let me think about it."

"Buy you a new smoke detector," he said enticingly.

She tipped her head up, smiling at him. Sean felt his heart reel in his chest. "You already promised that."

"Guess it's time to get more creative, huh? Tell you what." He slipped his arm around her shoulder. "How 'bout I come up with some great way to make my deception up to you, and in return you agree to have dinner with me one night?"

"I'll think about it," Gemma said lightly, ducking out of his embrace.

Sean grinned, shaking his head. "You're torturing me on purpose, aren't you?"

"Torture? *Moi?*"

"Then say yes to dinner with me."

"I'll think about it," Gemma promised. "After you surprise me."

The next morning, Gemma slid into her regular booth at the Happy Fork and waited for Stavros to come and harass her. She hadn't gotten any sleep; instead, she had lain awake thinking about Sean: Sean kissing her, Sean

peeling off her clothing, Sean whispering in her ear all
the things he wanted to do to her. She was glad when
Frankie appeared. She was bursting with the need to talk
about him.

Before she could get a word in, Stavros appeared, pouring Frankie's coffee and then depositing an empty coffee
cup in front of Gemma. He passed the steaming pot back
and forth beneath her nose.

"Smells good, no?"

"Smells great," Gemma concurred. "Pour me a cup."

Stavros and Frankie exchanged shocked glances as
Stavros complied.

"Sugar?" he asked in a stunned voice. "Cream?"

Gemma nodded. "Both."

Looking as if he might pass out, Stavros ran to fetch
them for her.

"If this isn't a sign of imminent apocalypse, I don't
know what is," said Frankie.

"No apocalypse," Gemma rejoined gaily. "I'm just up
for trying new things."

Frankie caught her drift and her arm shot across the
table. "Don't start yet; here comes Stavros with your milk
and cream."

His demeanor was now obsequious, as if Gemma were
a queen whose pronouncement he awaited. She fixed her
coffee and, with Stavros and Frankie both looking on intently, raised it to her lips.

"Well?" he asked.

"Best coffee I've ever tasted."

"Ha!" Stavros beamed down at her knowingly. "I knew
that would be your answer! Hasn't Stavros been telling
you this for years?"

"You have," Gemma admitted.

He waddled off looking as if he'd just won the lottery.

"What's going on?" Frankie demanded.

First she told Frankie about the firefighters coming to

her apartment. Then she told her about the hockey game. She finished with details of Domenica's christening party. Frankie practically lunged across the table.

"You've crossed paths with this guy three times?" she said excitedly. "And he has blue eyes?"

"Yes."

"Like in your vision?"

"Yup."

"You think—?"

"I don't know." For the first time, Gemma felt uncertain. "I want it to be. I think." She drank some coffee. "He asked me out to dinner," she added shyly.

Frankie's eyes bulged so far out she looked like a cartoon. "And you said no?"

"I said maybe."

"*Maybe?* Why? Because Venus isn't in the third house of Lexus or some crap like that?" Frankie eyed her critically. "Something else is going on here. Why don't you want to go out with this guy?"

Gemma peered at Frankie over the rim her coffee cup. "If I tell you, do you promise not to laugh?"

"No. Now tell me."

"I think I'm a little nervous about going out with him because he's a firefighter."

"What's that got to do with anything?"

"They're tribal."

"Excuse me? You come from an Italian family where two brothers married two sisters and you're worrying about tribal?"

"That's different," Gemma insisted. "Look, I know they're heroes, okay? I know what they do is dangerous. I respect that." She ran a thumb along her napkin. "But remember the neighborhood firehouse in Brooklyn? Remember how those guys used to sit outside and call out rude things to us when we'd walk by on the way home from school?"

Frankie cringed. "Remember that time they rated us like they were Olympic judges and held up number cards?"

"Yeah, and gave us both zeroes." The memory still stung. "Remember how drunk they'd all get on St. Patrick's Day, spilling out onto the streets singing 'Danny Boy' and 'A Nation Once Again'?" Gemma shuddered. "That's not a tribe I want to be part of."

"Just because he's a fireman doesn't mean he acts that way."

"You're right. Though he was pounding down the Guinness at the christening party."

Frankie frowned. "Pounding down or had a couple? Which is it?"

"Had a couple," Gemma mumbled.

"Oohh, what a sin, a man having a few beers at a party. Better drag his ass to AA right now."

Gemma smiled at her friend affectionately. "You're a bitch, you know that?"

"I'm your favorite bitch and don't you forget it. Give this guy a chance. Please. I think he's got real potential."

"We'll see, okay? We'll see." Gemma was eager to get off the topic of Sean. "How's your flesh-eating disease?"

"The mental fuzziness and blister seem to have disappeared on their own," Frankie admitted sheepishly. "But now I have this." She lifted the pale blond bangs off her forehead to reveal . . . nothing.

"What?"

"I'm going bald, Gemma." Frankie's voice was laced with despair. "Look at my hairline! It's receding."

"The only thing receding is your grip on reality. I swear to God, you have got to talk to someone about your hypochondria. It's not healthy."

"I'll talk to someone about my 'hypochondria' when you talk to someone about why you're hesitating over gorgeous guy who's obviously been put in your path. Sound fair?"

Gemma squirmed. "Stavros! More coffee!"

"Croppy's having a shit fit."

Tony the doorman's usual greeting was, "Hey, Short-stuff, what's up?" The words "Croppy" and "shit fit" were not words Gemma wanted to hear at the end of a long day.

"What's going on?" she asked as she put down her grocery bags.

"She's complained to the super twice about the junk outside your door. Says it's blocking the hall. It's a fire hazard."

"I don't have any junk in the hall."

"Croppy says you do." His tone was exasperated. "Do me a favor, will you? Whatever it is, whether it's yours or not, could you get rid of it? She's a pain in the ass. That's the only way she'll ever shut up."

"Not a problem," Gemma assured him. According to Mrs. Croppy, Gemma was responsible when the hot water didn't work, when the kids in the apartment upstairs blasted the TV, and when the elevator was out of order. *She probably thinks I'm responsible for global warming, too.*

"Thanks, Gemma. Have a good night."

"You too."

Since the grocery bags were unwieldy, Gemma asked another woman boarding the elevator to please press the button for the fifth floor. The woman complied, pressing the buttons for both five and twelve.

The doors opened on the fifth floor, and Gemma stepped out into the hall. She hadn't taken three steps before the door to Mrs. Croppy's apartment flew open. The old woman was hurtling toward her like one of the Furies, her shrill voice loud enough for the entire floor to hear.

"You! I've been waiting for you all day! Your junk is littering the hallway! People can't walk! It's dangerous!"

"What are you talking about?" Gemma tried to make her way down the hall. Her bags were getting heavier with every step. If she didn't put them down soon, they'd slip from her hands.

"Look! " Mrs. Croppy squawked, pointing a crooked, bejeweled finger at the other end of the hall. "Just look!"

Gemma wearily lowered the bags and looked. There, in front of her doorway and extending the entire width of the hall, was a menagerie of stuffed animals large and small. Penguins, polar bears, orangutans, rhinos—every animal imaginable, their colors as vivid as a rainbow.

"Oh my God," Gemma whispered, transfixed. Mrs. Croppy was still screeching, but Gemma had stopped listening. Slowly, as if in a dream, she made her way toward her apartment. Tigers, elephants, woodchucks—she was ankle deep in faux wildlife, the soft synthetic fur of zebras and raccoons brushing her skin as she fumbled to open the door of her apartment.

"What are you going to do about this mess?" Mrs. Croppy squawked.

Gemma barely heard the poison in the old woman's voice. "Just give me a minute, okay?"

Mrs. Croppy grunted and slammed her door shut, leaving Gemma in blessed silence. She knew just what she'd do. First, she'd dump her groceries on the kitchen table. Then she'd move her furry friends inside. And then—dear God, how she wanted to shout out his name!—then she would go upstairs and pay a visit to Sean.

Sean smiled when the doorbell rang, knowing just who it was. The electronic chime made Pete and Roger hop excitedly on their perches and they began squawking. Not the most relaxing sound in the world, but he was used to it.

"Settle down, guys," he soothed as he opened the door to reveal Gemma.

"Hi," she said shyly.

"Hi," he returned, ushering her inside and closing the door.

Gemma's gaze covered every inch of his living room: the dusty bookshelves crammed with his history books and spy novels; his coffee table, which held the latest issue of *Firehouse* magazine.

His gaze, meanwhile, was riveted on her. Her curling red hair looked windswept, and she was wearing the same scent as at the christening, faintly floral, but with a hint of spice that stirred his blood. His mind kept flashing back to the teddy on her bed, then flashing forward to an image of her in it. No one had ever captivated him so thoroughly, so fast. He felt bewitched.

"Care to introduce me to your roommates?" she asked, her gaze coming to rest on his birds.

They crossed the room, approaching the twin cages. "This is Pete and this is Roger. Pete is a parakeet, and Roger is a cockatiel."

As if they sensed they were the subject of conversation, the birds squawked even louder. Gemma leaned in to get a closer look at them, especially Roger, who boasted a small patch of orange feathers on his chest.

"You rescued them?"

"Yeah, from a fire in a dry-cleaning store, of all places. After the fire the owner went back to Korea and I took them."

"His loss." She tilted her head this way and that, observing them from different angles. "They're pretty."

"Pretty neurotic. Sometimes the only way I can get Rog to calm down is to pace with him, like a baby."

"Interesting." She turned to him, her smile shy. "Thank you."

"For—?" he asked, pretending he didn't understand.

She jostled his arm playfully. "You know what for. I love them."

"I'm glad. You have no idea how hard it was finding a pink wildebeest." Outwardly he was cracking jokes, but inside, he felt pure relief. It had been a gamble: Either she'd love it, or she'd think he was a nut. Lucky for him, it was the former. "Does this mean I'm forgiven for my deception?"

"I don't know," Gemma teased. "One of my neighbors was pretty upset."

Sean frowned. "Croppy, right?"

"Yes! How did you know?"

"The woman's a professional ball buster. Take off those orthopedic shoes of hers and you'll find cloven hooves."

Gemma laughed.

"I like making you laugh. C'mere."

As smoothly as he could, he took her face in his hands and, with the care of an artist, brushed his lips over hers once, then twice. Teasing kisses, nothing too forceful, just a taste of what could come should Gemma desire more. "More?"

Gemma's smile was demure yet seductive. "Yes, please."

"FDNY at your service, miss," he breathed, crushing his mouth down on hers as his arms drew her in tight. Through the soft crush of her breasts against his chest, he could feel her heart beating as fast as his own. He pressed on, feasting on the sweetness of her mouth. What was it about this woman that bewitched him so?

"Stop."

Stunned, Sean lifted his burning lips from Gemma's, and cleared his throat. "Stop?"

"Yes." Gemma gazed up into his face sheepishly. "I can't do this with them"—her voice dropped down to a whisper as her eyes slid quickly to his birds—"watching."

"You're kidding."

"I'm not. Their little eyes are glued to us." She gave a small shudder. "It's avian voyeurism!"

"I'll cover their cages. Or"—his thumb traced the plump curve of her lower lip, shocking even himself—"We can go into the other room."

Gemma hesitated. She was attracted to this man—very attracted. But she wasn't the sort to sleep with someone on the first date. Then again, this wasn't really a date, right? And she was a grown woman. She closed her eyes for a moment, trying to fully take in all she was feeling. "Can we go downstairs to my place?" she murmured.

"Of course."

She opened her eyes to look up into his. There she saw the deep, perfect blue of a Caribbean sea in which she longed to drown. Life without risk was no life at all. And since she was the one who was always telling others to have faith, it was time to practice what she preached.

She took his hand.

"Follow me," she said.

Gemma led Sean into her apartment. Since they were at her place, at her suggestion, she was now the one responsible for seduction. She went to light the candles scattered around her living room, hoping she appeared nonchalant, even serene. Part of her wanted to be the one in control: to show him how beguiling she could be, how powerfully she could enchant using the untapped magic of the senses. But another part wanted to be the one who surrendered, to be guided by this man to the place where she could soar free of the confines of her body, experiencing the past, present, and future in the simplicity of a single kiss.

Candles lit, she turned back to Sean, expecting to find him where she'd left him, standing near the front door. But he wasn't there. Instead, he was standing in the doorway of her bedroom, right hand held out to hers in unmistakable invitation.

"What are you doing there?" Gemma asked coyly as she walked toward him, kicking off her shoes along the way. Sean did the same.

"Checking to see if you'd gotten that new smoke detector."

"I thought you were getting one for me."

"Only if you're a good girl."

"I'd much prefer being a bad one, Mr. Kennealy."

"Prove it. Put on that black teddy of yours."

"That can be arranged." She nudged him gently in the direction of the bedroom door. "Give me a minute."

"Certainly."

Alone, Gemma paused to catch her breath. His request excited her more than she thought possible; a total rush of anticipation was twisting its way through her, delectable yet maddening. Trembling, she quickly shucked her clothing and took the teddy out of her dresser. She slipped it on, reveling in the soft feeling of the silk upon her bare skin. Tousling her hair for good measure, she threw back her shoulders, pushed her cleavage forward, and flung open the bedroom door.

There was Sean, restless, waiting, desire for her shining in his eyes. Drinking her in, he smiled. Candlelight suited him: The handsome angles of his face were made more so by the soft glow warming the room. Twining her fingers lightly through his, Gemma began pulling him toward a sea of oversized silk pillows arranged on the floor.

"No bedroom?"

Gemma smiled, catlike, and shook her head. Making love in the bedroom was predictable, and predictable was the last thing she wanted this experience to be. She wanted him left speechless, the memory of their coming together seared into his brain. She wanted him to want more.

"Come," she whispered, bidding him to sink down on the pillows with her.

"This is interesting," Sean observed. Gemma's reply was a smoldering smile and a swift, lusty nip to his lower lip. Sean's head jerked back slightly, eyes swallowed up by surprise. Whatever he'd been expecting, it certainly wasn't that. But she could see he liked it. Surprise gave way to animal drive and he clutched her to him.

"You sure this is how you want it?" he growled, his breath hot as he teased her earlobe with the tip of his tongue.

"No." It was hard to think straight. "I mean yes. I mean—"

His mouth silenced her, pressing upon hers with such fire, such demand, that Gemma could feel her body sizzling away, taking the last remnants of rational thought with it. There was only this: complete and total surrender to the sensual, spurred on by the thirst for more. She heard a voice crooning *yes, yes!* and it was a few seconds before she realized it was her own. Sean rewarded her begging with roughness, his teeth nipping and scraping so expertly that Gemma found herself gasping as golden heat shattered her core. She would go mad if she didn't learn every inch of his body, feel his burning skin beneath the soft pads of her fingertips. One minute she was clutching him tight, the next she was caressing his hair, his soft black curls a gift in her hands. She ached for more than simply being with him; she wanted to become him, to not be able to detect where he left off and she began.

His mouth's fierce demands left her lips bruised and swollen. Suns exploded behind the closed lids of her eyes, pleasure sluicing its way through her body like a river. All he demanded she would willingly give, and more. The harder he kissed, the more fervently his fingers explored, the deeper she dug her nails into the muscled terrain of his back. She was an animal, an animal whose blood and bone and sex beat out only one thought: More. More. More.

Breath ragged, Sean lifted his head, his wild eyes meeting hers. There was no need for words. Every need was conveyed in a glance. He tugged at the thin straps of her teddy, desperate for the softness beneath. Gemma helped him and held her breath, back arching as Sean lowered his mouth to her heated flesh.

Sean's tongue flicked and teased. His hands roughly explored her body—squeezing, probing, kneading—each sensation provoking in her a new round of blind arousal. She wanted him soon. She wanted him now. She needed to wrest back control.

Forcing his head up, she began frantically unbuttoning his shirt. He pushed her back down among the pillows and tore her teddy away from her body, the sound of ripping silk the most seductive music on earth. Gemma felt her own wet heat between her legs.

"Which of us is in charge?" Sean demanded hoarsely.

"You," Gemma moaned, dizzily ceding control. "You."

Nodding, Sean hurried to free himself, his breath hitching as his eyes locked on hers. Naked, he climbed atop her, fingers grasping her hips, hard, as Gemma arched upward, opening herself to him. He paused over her a moment and then plunged hard and deep, Gemma catapulting over the edge as their bodies began moving together, her dream of melding into one coming true.

His thrusting was strong and sure. Gemma tightened herself around him as he drove into her again and again, each meeting of flesh upon flesh pushing her higher and higher into the stratosphere. One minute she was a sweet prisoner of her body, her shocked senses unable to catalog the firestorm of relentless sensations coming one after another after another; the next she was flying, her body just a memory as she bucked wildly beneath him. It was a sensation she never wanted to end.

Gemma smiled with pleasure as Sean's body tensed and began moving faster, slamming itself into hers with an abandon that left her breathless. His desire for release was so urgent the expression on his face resembled pain. His hands searched for hers, their fingers twining together tight. *Now! Now! Now!* she thought feverishly, delighted when the drumming between her own legs resumed, sharp and insistent. Together they rode the storm their bodies created. And when he came—when they both came—a happiness she had never thought possible surged through her.

Her spell had worked.

She had found her soul mate.

CHAPTER
05

"What does your tattoo mean?"

Adrift on a cloud of postcoital bliss, Gemma languidly turned to Sean, in whose arms she lay. His thick curls were tousled wildly and his body boasted a thin sheen of sweat that made his flesh glisten in the candlelight. He looked like a warrior back from battle, weary yet triumphant, and very sexy. She'd been wondering when he'd notice the delicate tattoo gracing the small of her back. A small purple full moon framed by two opposite facing crescent moons, it was a present she'd given herself for her thirtieth birthday.

"It's a symbol of the goddess," she answered softly. Was the conversation about being a witch going to happen here, now, when they were both naked and vulnerable? Why not?

If Sean was baffled or curious, it didn't show. He nodded slowly as if mulling it over. Then he slid down her body, kissed the tattoo, and slid back up, holding her tight in his arms.

"I think tattoos on women are sexy."

"I'm glad," Gemma purred, trailing her fingers along the strong muscles of his damp back.

He grimaced. "I also think if we don't get off the floor soon, you'll need to call EMS. My back is killing me. Can we shift to the bed?"

Gemma chuckled. She was feeling uncomfortable herself. During their fierce lovemaking, the pillows she had so artfully arranged had slid, leaving the two of them lying on the bare wooden floor. Bed, with its promise of clean sheets and body-hugging blankets, seemed a wonderful suggestion. They could curl up together, maybe even make love again. In the morning they could go out for breakfast.

Gemma kissed his shoulder. "Bed sounds like a great idea." She stretched, surprised when it generated a small, sharp pain in her left shoulder. "I'm stiff, too."

"I guess this is what happens after thirty."

"Yoga helps."

"I'll stick to Advil."

His affectionate smile made Gemma's heart dance. Kissing the top of her head, he rose to his feet, extending his hand. Gemma took it, marveling at how easy this all felt, how natural, sharing her body with this man and now being led to her own bed. Hand in hand, they walked past the parade of stuffed animals, Sean pausing to pat the stuffed wildebeest on the head as if it were a faithful pet.

"Can I stay the night?" he asked as they burrowed beneath the covers.

Gemma nodded yes, burying her head in his neck. If she had her way, he'd never leave.

Sean didn't believe in fate. Yet there was something magical in the way their bodies had so smoothly blended together, a sense that this was meant to be. How else to explain his need to seduce this woman so quickly?

And she had a tattoo!

"A symbol of the goddess," she'd said. He knew a lot of women nowadays were into goddess worship. Not only had he read about it, but one of the guys he used to work with on Wall Street, Darryl Armbruster, was married to a woman who'd started out Catholic, gone Buddhist for a couple of years, and eventually wound up in some kind of all-girl coven. Armbruster used to bitch about coming home on the full moon to find his McMansion in Sommerville filled with chanting women. He glanced down at Gemma, who was sleeping peacefully. Could he picture her doing that? His gut tightened a little as he realized the answer was yes.

He continued watching her, her breath coming in short little puffs, the tangled mop of red hair curling wildly around her face. He envied her ability to just drift off. His rumbling belly kept him awake. He decided to go make himself a snack.

He gingerly slid out from between the sheets and made his way to the kitchen. He switched on the light, blinking against the momentary harshness. The feel of cold tile shocked the soles of his feet. *Pretty weird standing naked in someone else's kitchen,* he thought. Gemma's fridge held lots of salad and yogurt. He hated yogurt. Disappointed, he shut the door, and got a drink of water. Then he started opening cabinets, delighted to find Irish Breakfast tea among the boxes of herbal tea. A peek into the tiny pantry revealed a half-empty box of chocolate graham crackers just begging to be liberated. He put on her electric kettle. The appliance interested him; the only other person he knew to have one was his mother.

Waiting for the water to boil, Sean took in his surroundings. Her kitchen was small, but clean. Bundles of dried herbs hung from the ceiling in a corner of the room, and on the kitchen table sat an unopened box from Amazon.com. Curiosity drove him to check out the other bedroom. Turning on the light, he saw the room was basically bare, apart from an odd little table at its center and a bunch of giant candlesticks. Drawing close to the table, he saw a goblet, a white-handled knife, and a small bowl filled with ashes. There were also fresh flowers, two candles, and an old cracked, five-pointed star. He picked it up and turned it over in his hands. He'd seen these stars before. They had to do with heavy metal music or Satanism, he thought to himself grimly. Mildly perturbed, he tossed the star back onto the small table. What was the deal with the white-handled knife? The kettle buzzed and he jumped.

"Sean?"

He'd woken her up.

"Just making some tea," he called out. He turned off the kettle and poured the hot water into the cup. His chest now felt tight with anxiety. Between the vegetarianism, the herbs, and now this, he was having a hard time picturing Gemma hanging out with his friends. She just didn't fit in. Not only that, but she owned her own business. Were he still a stockbroker, it wouldn't be a problem. But some of the guys at the firehouse could be real pricks about this stuff. He could hear it already: You pussy-whipped, Kennealy? Does she give you an allowance? She your sugar mama or what?

"Can you bring me some, too?" Gemma called.

"Sure," he replied, forcing himself to sound calm.

"Bengal spice, please."

"You got it."

He extracted another cup from the cupboard as well as the tea in question. Tea steeped and ready, he picked up both steaming mugs and started back to the bedroom, acutely aware of his nakedness. He felt like the butler in a porn film.

Propped up in bed, Gemma smiled as Sean came through the bedroom door nude bearing two cups of tea. "You should have woken me," she said, eyes following him as he sat down atop the covers beside her. "I could have fixed you something."

"What? Yogurt pie? All you've got is yogurt and graham crackers."

"I'm sorry. I wasn't expecting company. We could order in; the Indian place around the corner doesn't close until one A.M."

"If I eat Indian food at this hour, I'll be up all night with heartburn." He shook his head, biting into one of the graham crackers he'd brought with him. "This'll tide me over."

Gemma sipped her tea, the taste of cinnamon and cardamom making her mouth tingle. She turned to thank him; that's when she noticed the pensive look in his eyes.

"Sean? Are you okay?"

He peered at her as if he needed to make out more clearly whom he was speaking to. "Yeah. I just . . ."

"What?"

Sean drew a deep breath. "While the water was boiling, I looked around the apartment and found—"

"My altar," Gemma finished for him, leaning back against the wall of pillows.

"Yeah." His expression was troubled. "You don't put dresses on cats and sacrifice them, do you?"

"What?" Gemma broke into laughter. "No! I practice Wicca, Sean. I'm not into Voodoo or Satanism."

"Wicca," he repeated.

"It's an earth-based, Pagan religion," she began explaining.

"I know what it is," he cut in impatiently. "It means you're a witch. Should I call you Sabrina or Samantha?"

"Neither. I don't wiggle my nose and turn people into bunnies. I do not own a black cat, a broomstick, or a big black hat."

Sean rubbed his forehead. "And your store?"

"What about it?"

"What do you sell?"

"Books and occult supplies."

Sean groaned.

"What? What's wrong?"

"It's nothing. Just forget it."

Gemma hopped out of bed, putting on her kimono. "You're completely weirded out, aren't you?" she sighed, settling down next to him.

"I guess." Sean peered at her nervously. "Are you in a coven?"

"No. I like to worship on my own." She seemed somewhat bemused. "Anything else you want to know?"

"Anything else you want to tell me?"

"Hhmm, let me think." Gemma rested her head on his shoulder. "Well, my best friend is a DJ and I give tarot card lessons."

"Great," Sean muttered.

Gemma lifted her head slowly and looked at him. "I'm the same person I was an hour ago, Sean. Nothing's changed."

"Except you might turn me into a toad."

She elbowed him in the ribs affectionately. "Don't be an ass." Taking the teacup from his hand, she put it on the nightstand with her own. Then she wrapped her arms around him.

"Ask me anything," she murmured tenderly. "I'm not embarrassed or shy about anything in my life. In fact, I'm pretty proud of the life I lead."

Lightening up a little, Sean kissed her forehead. "At least we've got that in common."

Trying to recapture the magic he'd felt earlier in the evening, he lay down with her, plying her with questions. She told him about the Golden Bough, and how happy she was to be able to run a business that reflected her beliefs. About Frankie, and how they'd known each other since they were little girls. Finally she talked about her family, and how much she loved them. Time passed, and their tea grew cold. Eventually, to Sean's relief, Gemma fell asleep.

"Sean?" Gemma reached out to touch the body slumbering beside her. But there was only a tangle of sheets and an empty pillow. Concerned, she switched on the light. The clock on the nightstand read 4:00 A.M. Maybe he was in the bathroom?

She waited a few minutes, determined not to immediately assume the worst. Donning her kimono, she made her way out into the silent living room and turned on the light.

That's when she saw it.

A note in the mouth of the stuffed wildebeest.

Back killing me.
Went to sleep on my own rock hard mattress.

She stared at it for a long time, then crumpled the note and let it drop to the floor. Picking up the wildebeest, she trudged back to her bedroom. The two cups of tea were still sitting there on the nightstand. Clutching the stuffed animal to her, she lay atop the covers, curling up in a ball. There were lots of ways to keep pain at bay; holding on tightly to something was one of them. It wasn't what she'd imagined holding through the night, but Sean had left her with no choice.

CHAPTER

06

"Birdman, you gonna take that lasagna out or what? It's startin' to smell like that warehouse fire on Forty-third."

It was Sean's turn to cook and he was making lasagna, tossed salad, and garlic bread. But Leary was right: He'd totally spaced on the lasagna, which now smelled more than well-done. Grabbing a pair of oven mitts, he hustled to the oven and opened the door. A wall of heat smacked him in the face, along with acrid smoke. The top of the lasagna was charred.

"Way to go, Chef Boyardee. Your head up your ass tonight or what?"

"Shoulda stuck with crunching numbers, boyo."

"Up yours," Sean called over his shoulder good-naturedly. His head was up his ass, it was true. But right now, his primary concern was salvaging dinner. He peeled the top layer off the lasagna and brought the rest to the table.

"You expect us to eat this?" Lieutenant Peter Carrey asked. Carrey had been with the FDNY for twenty years and was highly respected.

"Yeah, really," Leary echoed. "It's dryer than an AA meeting."

"You'd know all about that, Mikey, wouldn't ya?" Sal Ojeda ribbed.

"Damn straight. I've been free of Irish handcuffs for years."

Bill Donnelly looked at him questioningly. "Irish handcuffs?"

"Beer in each hand."

Everyone laughed.

Sean sat down beside Leary, who was eating like a man breaking a fast. "Not bad considering you burnt it to shit," he commented.

"Thanks," Sean said, taking a mouthful. Carrey was right: The lasagna was dry, but it wasn't inedible.

"So what's up with you?" Leary asked curiously. "You've looked like a zombie since you got here."

"Ah, it's nothing."

"C'mon, Sean." Leary draped an arm around Sean's shoulder. "Tell Uncle Mikey all your problems."

Sean hesitated. If he spilled, he wouldn't just be telling "Uncle Mikey," he'd be telling everyone on his shift. But maybe the more opinions he got, the better. "I met this girl, right?" Wolf whistles started immediately. Sean rolled his eyes. Maybe he didn't need more opinions.

"Go on, my son," said Leary solemnly, folding his hands on his chest in imitation of a priest hearing confession.

"She's kind of unusual."

" 'Unusual,' " Bill Donnelly snorted. "What the hell does that mean? She got three tits?"

Laughter erupted around the table.

"No, she's into herbs and stuff. She's a vegetarian." No way was he going to tell them she was a witch. Not now, at any rate.

"Lots of people are vegetarians these days," probie Ted Delaney said knowingly. "That's not so weird."

"She meditates." His eyes shot to Leary's. "She burns incense."

"Sweet mother o' God." Leary let out a whoop of disbelief. "It's The Stinker, isn't it?"

"The Stinker!" Joe Johnson, ladder truck chauffeur, looked shocked. "You mean, the loony who lives below you who was burning garbage?"

"She's not burning garbage," Sean clarified, sounding—and feeling—semimiserable. "It's incense."

"Incense that smells like Elizabeth, New Jersey, on a bad day," Leary added.

"You've been bitching about The Stinker for months, bro!" Ojeda pointed out.

Ted Delaney looked confused. "And now you like her?"

"Yeah. I mean—she's really nice. And sweet. But she's, you know, different."

"Different can be good," Joe Johnson opined. "My wife changed her hair color last week. She looks ten years younger."

"We're talking about a woman here, you moron, not the pros and cons of Clairol." Leary gave Sean a penetrating look. "You've talked to her since—?"

Sean gave a quick nod. "Yeah. And we get along really well. But she's quirky. I mean, I told her about eating smoke and getting headaches and she told me to chew on some kind of root."

"Bet you want her to chew on your root," Ojeda cracked.

Sean seared him with a look and Ojeda slumped in his seat. The innuendo served only to remind Sean of how ungallantly he'd behaved. He had woken up in a room that wasn't his own with the backache from hell, beside a woman with an altar and a ritual knife, and his reflex was to run. So he left. It wasn't until he was stretched out in his own bed that it crossed his mind how Gemma might feel, waking up to an empty bed and a hastily scribbled note.

"Here's some food for thought, Kennealy."

Sean turned to the far end of the table, where Chris "Socrates" Campbell sat. Socrates had earned his nickname because he felt compelled to add what he thought were insightful comments to any conversation. Sometimes they actually *were* insightful.

"If you like this woman, what do you care if she's different?"

Because if there's one thing I want, it's to continue fitting in. I want to be normal, Sean answered to himself. Hooking up with a witch who ran an occult shop was not a smooth fit for the company's summer barbecues. Still, Socrates had a point.

"*Am I doing* this right?"

Uther Abramowitz's reedy voice brought Gemma back to herself. They were in her store, nearly done with his first tarot lesson, and somewhere between explaining to him why he needed to learn the meaning of each card and showing him how to do a three-card spread, her mind had drifted back to her night with Sean. The neediness in Uther's voice made her feel guilty. Here he was paying her money to learn tarot, and what was she doing? Daydreaming. Gently removing the tarot deck from his grasp, Gemma showed him again what to do.

"You shuffle the deck, and then you ask the querent— remember, that's the person who wants the reading—to cut the deck into thirds with his left hand. Then have them turn over the top three cards, and put them in any order they want. The first card denotes the past, the second the present, the third the future. This reading is good for someone who wants a specific question answered. You can also do the one card read I showed you earlier."

Uther stroked his straggly beard. "Can we tr͏̵ mean—can I ask a question and see what happens?"

"Of course."

Gemma handed him the deck, unprepared for the di͏̵ rectness in his eyes as he shuffled the deck.

"Will I ever find my lady love?" he intoned solemnly, staring straight at her.

"You don't have to ask the question out loud."

"Oh."

Uther shuffled . . . and shuffled . . . and shuffled, giving Gemma time to process the fact that he obviously had a crush on her. This wasn't good.

"Done."

Excited as a child completing his first finger painting, Uther turned over the top card. It was the Nine of Swords. *Damn*, thought Gemma.

"Do you know what card it is?" she prompted.

Uther's scrawny chest puffed up. "Nine of swords, obviously."

Gemma nodded approvingly. "Any idea what it signifies?"

"You tell me." His gaze hinted at seduction. "I am but your humble pupil, Lady, and hope always to be."

"It's symbolic of suffering," Gemma explained, ignoring his lame, faux-Shakespearean attempt at flirting. "Patient suffering that has to be borne with courage."

Uther deflated. "Oh."

"It's not absolute, you know," Gemma reminded him. Much as his blatant staring was beginning to unnerve her, she still felt sorry for the guy. He was obviously lonely. She tried to think if she had any girlfriends she might hook him up with, but came up blank.

"We need to wrap up," she told him. "The hour's up and I need to reopen my store."

"Okay." Uther looked almost petulant. "What task hast thou set for me this week?"

eaning of any five cards you want."

o more, you know. I have a photo-

arn the meaning for all the cards."

. He looked uncertain.

nat was a joke, Uther. Learn at least five, and if you want to do more, feel free."

"Will do, Lady Most Fair. Mind if I look around the store awhile after you reopen?"

"Be my guest." Gemma slid out from behind the counter. "Oh, and Uther?"

She was going to tell him to can the poesy or he'd find himself not with Lady Fair but Lady Macbeth, but stopped herself. "Enjoy the rest of your day."

It embarrassed Sean, but to find Gemma's store he had to look Thompson Street up on a map. Like the area surrounding Wall Street where he'd once worked, the Village was filled with narrow, twisting streets, so different from the rigid grid system upon which the rest of Manhattan was mapped. Bleecker, Houston, Broome, Canal—Sean was familiar with the names, but had never hung out there himself.

He came up out of the subway on West Fourth Street, map in hand, looking like a tourist. It took a while, but he finally found the Golden Bough, right off the intersection of Thompson and Grand. Part of him expected something dark and Dickensian, with a black cat sitting in the store window atop a pile of dusty books. Instead, he found a small but bright shop whose sign blazed in gold and purple. The window display was pleasantly busy with books, tarots cards, crystals, and candles. Doubt crept in as he gripped the door handle. *Do I really want to do this?*

He paused, recalling Socrates Campbell's words of wisdom. So what if Gemma was different? Wasn't that what had attracted him to her in the first place? To automatically assume she wouldn't fit in was narrow-minded and ignorant, two adjectives he didn't want applied to him. At the very least, he owed Gemma an apology. In the best of all possible worlds, she would forgive him and maybe, just maybe, agree to a real date with him. Assuming she didn't catch sight of him and tell him to go to hell immediately. *Or send me there herself.*

He opened the door and slipped inside, gratified to see there were other customers in the store. The presence of other shoppers ensured she wouldn't wing things at him, call him names, and tear him a new one. He hoped.

The inside of the store was brightly lit and well organized, with a soothing aroma in the air that reminded him of Christmas trees. He recognized the music playing: Enya. His sister Christine threw her on the CD player at every family gathering. *So we both like Celtic music. That's a good sign, isn't it?*

Some customers were scrutinizing the tall bookshelves, while others sat in overstuffed chairs, leisurely thumbing through books. There was a welcoming feeling to the place that he realized reflected the warmth of the woman who owned the store. A quick peek up the "Reincarnation and Past Lives" aisle revealed Gemma sitting behind the counter, talking quietly to some skinny, bearded man who looked like he could use a strong dose of sunlight. Grateful she hadn't noticed him yet, Sean hung back, waiting until she finished. Her back was turned to him as she said goodbye to the man, who threw Sean a dirty look as he crept past him on his way out of the store.

"Excuse me, miss, I need your help finding a book."

Gemma jerked around. Sean saw shock in her eyes that quickly turned to distrust. He could see how much damage he'd done.

"What kind of book are you looking for?" She smelled

sweetly of the same perfume she'd worn at the christening, but spoke politely, as if to a stranger.

"A primer on Wicca."

"I see." Her expression betrayed nothing. "Follow me."

Slipping out from behind the counter, she walked briskly down one of the tall aisles. Sean followed at a slight distance. Was this how it was going to be, shopkeeper and customer? The next move, he realized, was his.

Within seconds Gemma pulled a book off the shelf, handing it to him. "This is good for beginners."

Sean skimmed the cover. *The Complete Idiot's Guide to Witchcraft.* "Complete idiot: That's me, all right. Thanks." He peered at her, hoping his joke might melt the ice.

"You're welcome." Turning heel, she walked back to the counter, barely looking at him when he handed her the book to ring up.

"That'll be ten ninety-five, plus tax."

Forget humor, proceed directly to shame, 'cause it's the only chance you've got. "Gemma, I came here to apologize."

She pointedly refused to look at him as she took his twenty dollars.

"It was a shitty thing to do," Sean said quietly.

Her eyes looked up at him sadly. "Yes, it was. It made me feel cheap. You think I do that all the time? Give myself away like that?"

"I'm sorry. That's not how I want you to feel. And it's not what I think, either."

"Well, that's a comfort. God knows I've spent the past week worrying about what you think."

Sean flinched at her sarcasm. "I deserved that. Hit me again."

"I don't want to hit you again." Her voice was shaky "Look, we slept together, it was a mistake, now let's move on."

She moved to hand him his change. Sean's hand shot out, gripping hers.

"I don't think it was a mistake."

Gemma gently withdrew her hand. "Then why did you leave without saying a word?"

Sean glanced around to make sure none of the nearby patrons could hear him. "Because my back was killing me and I was scared. I meet someone really interesting and then she turns around and tells me she's a witch. Wouldn't you have been freaked out?"

"I wouldn't have gone snooping around in someone else's apartment."

"If I hadn't found your altar, you wouldn't have told me?"

Gemma looked dismayed. "Of course I would have told you. But in my own time, in my own way. I might even have waited until we both had clothes on."

Sean swallowed, embarrassed. "I'm sorry," he repeated after a long moment. "I'm sorry I was nosy. I'm sorry I put you on the spot at an awkward moment, and I'm sorry I crept out in the middle of the night like a slimeball."

"Apologies accepted," Gemma murmured reluctantly.

She'd forgiven him! He had to grab the opportunity to see her again. "I was thinking."

"That could be dangerous, but continue."

"You and I did things ass backwards." His voice dropped. "You know, having sex first and all that."

"And?"

"I thought maybe we could do things right, you know, spend some time together."

"And then have sex," Gemma added acidly.

"No." Sean was reeling. "Well—I mean—if you want." Gemma frowned. "You know, I don't usually hop into bed so quickly, either," Sean added.

"Oh, really." Gemma looked skeptical.

"Yeah, really. I'm not quite sure what happened between us. It felt magical. I know that's probably not a good word for me to use, but I don't know how else to describe it."

Gemma's face lit up with a little smile.

"What?"

"Nothing."

"So, you'll go out with me, then?"

"Depends what you have in mind." When Sean looked surprised, Gemma laughed. "What, did you just expect me to say 'Yes' without hesitation after what you did to me?"

Sean could feel his ears burning. "Uh . . ."

"You did, didn't you?"

"I did, yeah," he admitted, defending his title as Stupidest Man in the World.

Gemma folded her arms across her chest, chuckling. "That's pretty presumptuous, don't you think?"

"That's me, ole Mr. Presumption."

"Well, Mr. Presumption, tell me what you have in mind."

Sean thought quick. "How about we go out, grab a bite to eat, and listen to some Irish music? There's this great place called O'Toole's down by Met Gar."

Gemma nodded slowly. "Irish music . . . that could be fun."

Sean's heart leapt. "So is that a yes?"

"I guess," Gemma said, beginning to look like her old happy self.

As she prepared for her date with Sean, Gemma's imagination danced with all sorts of visions. She pictured them at one of the city's small, trendy bistros, murmuring intimately at a table for two. Afterward, they would walk hand in hand to O'Toole's, the night air invigorating and full of promise. Both would be moved to tears by the heartrending sound of the Irish penny whistle as it trilled mournfully behind a singer with streaming raven hair who sang of hurling herself into her lover's open grave. The evening would leave them feeling tender and emotional. They'd go back to Gemma's place and make slow, deliberate love.

Instead, Gemma found herself being led by the hand down narrow steps to a basement pub. Sean opened the door, and Gemma found herself up against a solid wall of human bodies. Gabbing loudly, many were well on the road to intoxication despite it being only 9 P.M. She glanced sideways at Sean to see if he found the scene as disconcerting as she did.

"The food here is fantastic," he shouted in her ear.

Apparently not.

Doing her best not to jostle pub patrons as she squeezed past, she let Sean lead her to the front of the room. The combination of tightly packed bodies and lack of ventilation had perspiration dripping down the black concrete walls. Gemma was glad she hadn't worn a long-sleeved blouse as planned. Ten minutes in this sweatbox and she'd be drenched.

"Wait until you hear the music," Sean said as he pulled out a chair for her at a small table for two marked RE- SERVED. She already heard music coming from the jukebox in the corner, its main melody muddied by the nonstop din of voices. She strained to make out the tune. Something by U2? Their table was situated right in front of the small stage. If Gemma pushed back too far in her chair, her back practically touched an amplifier. She touched Sean's arm.

"Do you think we could find a different table?" she asked loudly.

Sean surveyed the room. "I think this might be it."

Gemma did a quick circuit of the room. He was right. This was it.

Out of the whirlwind a waitress appeared, handing each of them a menu. "What can I get you to start?" she asked in an Irish brogue so thick Gemma thought she had to be putting it on.

"A Guinness," Sean replied easily. The waitress turned to Gemma expectantly.

"Gin and tonic, please."

"Made with Tanqueray," Sean added. The waitress nodded and disappeared into the crowd.

"How do you know this place?" Gemma asked.

"It's a popular FDNY hangout." He glanced around the room. "I'm surprised no one I know is here."

Gemma suspected as much. She felt like a fish out of water. The last time she'd been in a place like this . . . wait: Had she ever been in a place like this?

Sean smiled at her, and she flipped open the menu, skimming the selections. Corned beef and cabbage. Bangers and mash. Fish and chips. Meat pies. Burgers. Gemma closed the menu.

"Know what you want already?"

"There's a small problem."

Sean dragged his chair closer to hers. Obviously he was having as tough a time hearing as she was. "What's that?"

"I'm a vegetarian, remember?"

"Shit. I didn't even think . . ." He trolled the menu, his easygoing expression slowly giving way to mild embarrassment.

"It's okay," Gemma assured him, squeezing his hand. "I'm sure I can find something." She leaned over so their shoulders were touching, taking another look at the menu. "There: cheese and onion pie. I'll have that."

Sean closed the menu, looking miserable. "I'm so sorry, Gem. I should have remembered."

"Not a big deal."

The waitress returned, plonking their drinks down on the table. "Do you know what you want, then?"

"I'll have the cheese and onion pie," said Gemma.

"Sorry, love, we're all out."

"Oh."

"Do you have any salads?" Sean asked.

The waitress bit down on the tip of her pen impatiently. "What you see on the menu is what you get. Sorry."

"In that case," said Gemma, "I guess I'll just have a plate of chips."

The waitress looked testy. "That's it? Chips?"

"Yes." Gemma shot Sean a baffled look.

"I'm not sure you can do that, you know. Just have chips."

"Oh," Gemma repeated, confused. "Why not?"

"Because chips *go with* something." The waitress clucked her tongue in frustration. "Fish and chips. Sausage and chips. We've never had anyone ask for 'just chips' before. I'll have to ask the chef if it's okay."

Gemma looked at the waitress warmly. "I'm sure it'll be fine."

"It might not be."

"Let's just see how it goes," Sean intervened, a big, fake smile cruising its way onto his face. It made Gemma want to laugh.

The waitress, now in a snit, peered down at Sean. "And what would you like, *sir?*"

"Bangers and mash, please." Sean closed his menu and handed it back with a knowing wink. "You can also tell the chef it's a New York City firefighter who wants that plate of chips."

"Very good," she bit out. "Thank you."

With that she left.

"Guess she doesn't care about getting a tip," Gemma joked.

"Customer service doesn't seem to be her strong point," Sean agreed.

Gemma sipped her drink. It was watered down, more tonic than gin. The evening was not starting out on the most auspicious note. Still, all might not be lost. So what

if O'Toole's was the kind of place she would never choose
to go to in a million years? The music was supposed to be
good, right? And there was Sean.

"How's your drink?" he asked, taking a pull of his
Guinness.

"Great," Gemma fibbed. "Yours?"

"Lovely," Sean said blissfully in a fake brogue.

"I've never understood the appeal of beer," Gemma admitted. "It's like"—she paused, searching for the right
analogy—"potato soda."

Sean laughed. "Spoken like a true beer connoisseur."

"So," Gemma began, permitting herself the great pleasure of gazing at long length into his incredible eyes, "have
you started to read the book on Wicca yet?"

Sean dipped his head, cupping his ear. "What?"

"The. Book. On. Wicca," she repeated loud and slow.
"Have you started it yet?"

"Yeah."

Gemma took this as a positive sign. "And—?"

"It's interesting."

She waited for him to elaborate, but he didn't. Gemma
could rattle off a slew of questions she was dying to ask
him about it, but she didn't want to make him feel pressured, or worse, that he was somehow being quizzed. Of
course, there was the possibility that he thought it was
bizarro mumbo jumbo and didn't want to hurt her feelings.
She was determined not to focus on that, not right now.
"How's work?" she asked brightly, practically shouting.

"Okay."

"Just okay? Any interesting fires?"

"They're all interesting. That's the problem." He
paused thoughtfully, then shrugged. "Things are fine.
Nothing exciting."

"I see."

"It's hard for me to talk about what I do, Gemma. If I
told you half the stuff that went down, you'd never want

me to leave my apartment, and the other stuff—the technical stuff—would probably bore you to tears."

"Try me," Gemma urged playfully. "What do you guys talk about? What do you do for fun?"

"Abuse each other." He took a sip of beer. "Wait, here's a good one: Some drunken teenager out on Long Island got stuck in the chimney of his frat house. By the time the fire department arrived, he was dead, unfortunately. Know what he died of?"

Gemma's hand flew to her throat. "What?"

"The flue." Sean laughed.

"Sean! That's not funny! That's awful!"

"Firehouse humor, babe. Sometimes it's the only thing that gets you through."

"I guess I can understand that," Gemma said. But deep down, she wondered.

The waitress returned with a smarmy look on her face and only one plate in her hand. She dropped the sausage and potatoes in front of Sean. "The chef said to tell ya, and I quote, that he doesn't give a flying feck if you're Mr. Jesus H. Christ himself, we only do what's on the menu."

"Bring us an order of sausage and chips, then," Sean said, slumping in his seat mortified. He turned to Gemma. "I'll take the sausages off the plate. So much for firefighters having some pull in this city," he added with a frown.

"We could go," Gemma suggested tentatively.

"But we haven't heard any music yet."

What does it matter? We'll be deaf by the time the band gets on, thought Gemma. The decibel level of the crowd was earthshaking. Still, Sean was right. They hadn't heard any live music yet. A few haunting Celtic ballads, a few foot-tapping ceilis, and the night would be back on track.

"Here, have some of these potatoes while we're waiting," Sean said, pushing his plate between them.

As delicately as she could, Gemma wiped away the perspiration she could feel beading on her upper lip. It was so

hot in O'Toole's she thought she might pass out. She tried
to see the place through Sean's eyes. Why had he had
brought her here? It had to be the music. The waitress
made a brief and unsmiling reappearance to drop the plate
of sausage and chips. Gemma and Sean tried to chat over
the raucous din; then just as they were finishing up their
meal, the lights dimmed and the crowd erupted into spontaneous hoots as the band hit the stage.

Gemma was expecting a quartet: fiddle, tin whistle, gui-
tar, and bodhran drum. Instead, eight musicians lumbered
onto the tiny stage. Two had fiddles and one had a tin whistle, but there was also a drummer, an organist, and much to
Gemma's dismay, a bass player and two electric guitarists,
one of whom plugged in to the amp at her back.

"Evenin'," the lead singer bellowed into the mike, a
pipe cleaner of a man with a buzz cut and black wrap-
around sunglasses. "We're deValera's Playground and
we'd like to start tonight with a little song you all know:
'Flogging Davy.'"

The nearest guitarist launched into a brain-searing riff
and the band were off. This was Irish music done a way
Gemma'd never heard, with screaming guitars vying with
mad fiddles and a lead singer who twitched and jerked like
Ichabod Crane being poked with a cattle prod. The crowd
was going nuts, pogoing in unison while their fists pumped
high in the air, shouting out the chorus in Gaelic along with
the band.

Gemma turned to Sean. He was clapping enthusiasti-
cally along with the music, which amazed her. Catching
her gaze, Sean broke into wide grin.

"AREN'T THEY GREAT?" he shouted.

"Great," Gemma mouthed, knowing he couldn't hear
her. As best she could, she averted her face from him so he
wouldn't detect her dismay. She'd been wrong: The music
wouldn't salvage this evening. Instead, it was the icing on
the cake. Time to face facts: Sean's idea of a fun night out

was radically different from hers. All she could do now was sit back and ride it out. She prayed the band did only one set and were either too drunk or tired to stand for encores. She wondered if Ron Crabnutt was somewhere in the crowd, chewing gum and waving a torx head in unison to the music.

And she wondered who Sean really was.

"Can I come in?"

The seductive undercurrent in Sean's voice as he teased Gemma's lips outside the door of her apartment almost caused her to give in. Almost. But then she remembered: This was the man to whom she'd given a second chance and he'd used it to take her to a rowdy Irish bar to see a band who played head-banging Celtic music. Now, to top it all off, he seemed to be hinting at sleeping with her again.

Gemma had been so sure that in agreeing to a proper date, she was sending a clear signal to him that she was interested in a relationship that existed beyond the boundaries of the bedroom. But now she wondered. Who did he think she was, that she would enjoy an evening like the one they'd just shared? Surprising her with all those stuffed animals had been wonderful, and his coming down to the Golden Bough to apologize to her in person spoke to his being a man of character. But if this was a firefighter's idea of a good date, then what she'd said to Frankie at the Happy Fork was right on target: This wasn't a tribe she wanted to join.

Maybe she was at fault, too. Just a little. When he'd asked her if she thought the band was great, she should have been honest and asked him to take her home. But she'd kept mum.

Gentle but firm, she pulled away. "I'm really tired, Sean. How about if we call it a night?"

"Okay." She saw disappointment as his eyes searched her face. "Are you all right?"

"Just tired," she repeated, turning her key in the lock.

"I hear you. What if I call you later in the week and we check out a movie?"

"That might be nice," Gemma murmured, pushing open her apartment door. She smiled up at him and thanked him for a lovely evening, happy when Sean planted a small, sweet kiss on her lips and thanked her for the same. But she could tell he was confused.

He wasn't the only one.

CHAPTER

07

His date with Gemma left Sean kicking himself.

He'd been so elated she was willing to give him another chance he'd grabbed at the first thing they seemed
to share: Irish music. O'Toole's sometimes *did* play traditional Irish music—he should have checked the paper
before heading down there. Judging by the music she
played in her store, it wasn't a stretch to think deValera's
Playground might not be her cup of tea. So he wasn't exactly surprised when she didn't invite him in afterward,
though he was disappointed. But what was with her tepid
response when he suggested a movie later in the week?
Did she really think it would be "nice" to get together
again? Or was she using polite Lady Speak to tell him to
go chase himself? Why did women have to be so damn
hard to read?

Rather than risk screwing up for a third and possibly
final time, Sean decided to consult someone who knew
Gemma well: her cousin Michael. Looking up the Blades
schedule online, he saw they were playing a home game,

and so he took the subway to Met Gar. His own experience with the FDNY team told him the Blades got there early to work on their sticks and skates. He told security he was a friend of Michael's, they checked with the man himself, and he was in.

The corridors below the arena were brightly lit and snaking, their concrete walls decorated with blown-up action photos of both past and present players. Sean found himself checking the sprinkler system on the ceiling, as well as the strategically placed fire extinguishers along the corridor. Funny the things you looked for depending on your point of reference.

He found Michael standing at one of the skate-sharpening machines, carefully running the blade of his skate back and forth, throwing off sparks.

"Mike."

"Hey, Sean." Michael put down his skate and drew him into a fraternal hug. "What's up? You boys need some tickets for tonight's game?"

"I hadn't come for that, but if you've got 'em, what the hell."

"Sure, I'll set you up. So, why you here?"

"It's about your cousin."

Michael looked amused. "Which one? I've got twenty."

Sean laughed appreciatively. "Gemma."

Concern flashed across Michael's face so fast Sean almost missed it. Was it possible Michael knew about the night they'd spent together? Had Gemma come crying to her cousin about what a creep he'd been? If so, then he was royally screwed. No way would Michael help him out.

"What about Gemma?" Michael asked carefully.

"I really like her. I took her out on Saturday, and it didn't go too well. I was hoping you might be able to give me some advice."

"I can try." Michael looked distinctly uneasy as he began massaging the back of his neck. "Look, before we go any further, there's some things you should probably know. About Gemma."

"Like what?" Sean could guess where this was heading, but he decided to play dumb. It would be fun watching Michael scramble to describe his cousin.

"Well, she's kinda crunchy, you know?"

"Crunchy?"

"Crunchy as in granola head. She's into herbs and teas and all that shit."

"I'm fine with that."

Michael's eyes darted away evasively. "She's also very spiritual, if you catch my drift. Intuitive. Very into nature."

"Tree hugger?"

"No, nothing like that. She's—"

"A witch?" Sean supplied.

Michael's eyes shot back to his. "*Madonn'*, she told you?"

Sean nodded.

"And it doesn't freak you out?"

Sean shuffled his feet evasively. "I don't really get it, but if it makes her happy . . ."

"My sentiments exactly," said Michael, looking relieved. "Hey, if you can get past the witch stuff, you're already light-years ahead of most guys. I salute you."

Sean frowned. "Don't salute me yet. I brought her to O'Toole's last week."

Michael's mouth fell open. "O'Toole's? Right around the corner?"

Sean nodded again, more forlorn this time.

"What are you, out of your fucking mind?"

"I know, I know," Sean muttered.

"Gemma at O'Toole's is like me rushing Kristie Yamaguchi. What the hell were you thinking?"

"I wanted to take her to see some Irish music."

"Who was playing?"

"DeValera's Playground." Sean sighed.

"They're good. Theresa's thinking of taking them on as clients. But no way are they up Gemma's alley."

"I know that now. She was playing Enya in the store so I just assumed she liked all sorts of Irish music."

Michael pulled a tortured face. "She loves that stuff."

"What stuff?"

"All that mystical Celtic crap. And traditional stuff, too." Michael shook his head despairingly. "I don't want to scare you, but once, when I was in the store, she was playing bagpipe music. What kind of Italian girl listens to freakin' bagpipes? I told her it was giving me a headache and she just ignored me. She marches to the sound of her own drummer."

"Yeah, she does," Sean agreed. *Which is kind of why I like her.* "Do you think she'd like it if I took her to hear traditional music?"

"Yeah, I do."

"Any other suggestions?"

Michael thought. "I think she'd like it if you cooked for her or something like that. She's kind of a homebody, you know? Likes quiet stuff." His hand shot out to clutch Sean's arm. "Don't ever get in a car with her, though. The woman can't drive to save her life."

Sean patted Michael on the shoulder. "Thanks for your help, Mike."

"No problem. I'll have some tickets put aside for you for tonight. Four okay?"

"Four's great. Thanks again," Sean repeated, starting down the hall. An idea was beginning to coalesce in his mind about what he could do to make Gemma feel excited about him again. It was a little offbeat, but so was she.

Besides, what did he have to lose?

"*You were at* O'Toole's? You?"

The incredulity in Frankie's voice made Gemma want

to yank off the hat she'd been wearing to cover her imaginary baldness and wing it to the kitchen floor. Gemma knew she wasn't ultrahip, but she wasn't a total geek, either. At least she didn't think she was.

"Why is that so hard to believe?"

"Because you're—you. You don't go to places like that."

"Yes, and if you'd been there Saturday night, you'd know why."

"Who was playing?" Frankie asked as she tucked in to her pasta.

"The Devil's Schoolyard. Something like that."

Frankie's fork halted in midair. "Do you mean deValera's Playground?"

"That's it."

"Oh my GOD! They're one of the hottest up-and-coming bands in New York! They're right on the verge of breaking out!"

Gemma filled her plate with salad. "That's nice."

"Were they great?"

"Frankie, they were awful. When Sean said we were going to hear Irish music, I expected to hear Irish music. Not screaming electric guitars and bongos."

"They're very eclectic. Big on the Afro-Celt scene. Did they do that rap song, 'Homey's Tipperary Crib'?"

Gemma took a sip of wine. "I think so. I'm not sure."

"Dinner's great," Frankie raved. "Thanks for inviting me." Helping herself to some garlic bread, she continued regarding Gemma with disbelief. "I can't *believe* you didn't like deValera's Playground. You need to expand your musical horizons, *señorita*."

"My horizons are wide enough, thank you very much." Recalling the evening made her melancholy. "Honestly, the night just went from bad to worse. What worries me is Sean thought it was fun."

"The world would be pretty damn boring if everyone liked the same thing, don't you think?"

Gemma paused to consider. "You're right. But"—she shifted uncomfortably in her chair, tucking her right leg beneath her—"what if his idea of fun and mine don't gel? I mean, I'm getting the idea that we move in . . ."

Gemma halted. A keening was coming from the street below.

"What the hell is that?" asked Frankie.

"Got me."

Both paused, listening for more. Gradually the sound began taking shape.

Bagpipes.

Intrigued, they ran to the bank of windows in Gemma's living room looking out on Fifty-ninth Street. There, on the sidewalk below, was Sean. With him were four bagpipers. Gemma recognized their bright red tunics and green-and-blue tartans from every photo she'd ever seen of a New York firefighter's funeral. They had to be members of the FDNY's Pipe and Drum Band.

"Oh my God," Gemma murmured to herself as they continued the lilting tune they were playing. Spotting her, Sean began waving like a lunatic.

Frankie turned to Gemma in alarm. "You know that guy?"

"That's Sean."

Frankie pressed her nose up against the glass for a better look, knocking her hat off her forehead. "He's hot, honey."

"Apparently he's also insane."

"He's motioning for you to open the window."

Gemma opened the window and leaned outside.

"Better than Saturday night, isn't it?" Sean yelled up to her over the din of the pipes.

"You're a madman!" she shouted back down to him, affection creeping into her voice.

"He's adorable," Frankie noted again with envy. "Not to mention creative."

But Gemma wasn't listening. Her mind was a-swirl with questions. How much was this costing him? How did he know she'd be home from work? How did he know she would like this?

Under any other circumstances, the thought of someone publicly serenading her might have embarrassed her. But this was different. This was extraordinary. Gemma closed her eyes, letting the haunting sounds of the pipes wash over her. She pictured herself surrounded by fields of green, golden sun pouring down on her face. And there, standing on a distant hillside beaming at her, was Sean.

"Care to come down?" his voice called up to her.

Gemma opened her eyes and turned to Frankie. "Do you think I should?"

"If you don't, I will. This guy's unbelievable!"

Gemma was inclined to agree. "I'm on my way," she shouted.

By now, a small crowd had gathered around Sean and the pipers, and traffic had slowed. People were hanging out the windows of surrounding apartment buildings, listening. Gemma made her way to Sean. The pipers had launched into "Danny Boy."

Sean's eyes danced with delight as Gemma joined him. "So, what do you think?"

"I think you're out of your mind. How much did this cost you?"

"Not much. A small donation." He pointed to the piper closest to him. "This is my brother-in-law, Tom." Tom gave a small wave. "He was helpful in putting this together." Sean took Gemma's elbow and steered her a few feet away from the four musicians, the better to talk. "There. Now we don't have to yell."

Boyish uncertainty took hold of Sean's face. "I know

you didn't have the best time Saturday night. I wanted to make it up to you."

Tenderness swept through Gemma. "You sure like to do things in a big way, don't you?" She smiled. "Suppose I hated bagpipe music?"

"I happen to know you don't."

"Oh?" Gemma playfully cocked her hip. "And how's that?"

"A certain hockey player told me."

Gemma couldn't hide her surprise. "This was Michael's idea?"

"No, this was my idea. But I thought I'd check first with someone who knew you well to find out your likes and dislikes."

"Uh-oh. What else did Michael say?" She knew what a wise-ass her cousin was. He probably told Sean she howled naked beneath the moon for fun or liked to spend Saturday nights growing mold specimens.

"He said you were kind of a homebody. Quiet. That you would probably like it if we stayed in and I cooked you dinner."

Gemma flushed with pleasure. "True."

"Good. Because here's what I was thinking." He came in closer, and Gemma's heart nearly burst right out of her chest. God, if only she could run her hands all over him right there on the sidewalk.

"Remember I told you I had a buddy in Long Beach who lets me use his apartment sometimes?" Gemma nodded. "Well, he's going away next weekend. And I thought—if it appealed to you, no pressure—we could spend the weekend there. We could take walks on the beach, I could cook for you, we could do other things . . ."

"Other things?" Gemma repeated softly, touching his arm.

"Well, yeah." Sean looked encouraged. "Sound good?"

"Sounds great." The mere thought of getting out of the

city for a few days made Gemma feel happy. "I'll just have to check with my part-timer to make sure she can cover the store." She clasped her hands together excitedly. "I've never stayed at the beach off-season!"

"You'll love it. Especially now that the summer crowds have left."

"I can't wait. We can take my car, if you want."

"No, that's okay," Sean said quickly. "I'll drive."

He said it so fast suspicion gripped Gemma, but she shrugged it off. "Fine with me."

The sound of the bagpipes faded away. Sean's brother-in-law lowered the instrument from his lips. "Need us to play anymore, Sean?"

Sean's gaze lit on Gemma, and held. "No, thanks, Tommy. I think you've done the trick."

Pristine white sand . . . endless blue horizon . . . wind kissing your face . . .

"I can see why you like to come here off-season," Gemma told Sean as they walked along the shoreline.

Sean gave her hand an appreciative squeeze. "After Labor Day weekend, it's like a switch gets thrown. All of a sudden, the crowds are gone, and Long Beach is just the locals and the birds."

Gemma followed his gaze, taking in the wide wooden boardwalk that seemed to go on for miles. A jogger made his way past the line of benches looking out to sea, while the center bike lane boasted an elderly couple cycling at a leisurely pace. A few feet beyond them, a young mother pushed a blond baby in a stroller, the infant blinking helplessly against the sun. Gemma turned her gaze back to the ocean. Lifting binoculars to her eyes, she zeroed in on a brown bird floating serenely on the waves, its bill tilted slightly upward.

"Do you know what kind of bird that is?"

Sean peered through her binoculars. "Common loon."

Gemma looked up into his face, so handsome in profile as he continued to study the sky. "I didn't know you knew so much about birds."

"It comes from goofing off in school," he confessed. "I was always looking out the window when I should have been paying attention. My teacher finally wised up, and had me write a report on all the different kinds of birds I saw. I guess the info stuck."

"Funny what sticks and what doesn't," Gemma mused. "Ask me who attended the First Continental Congress and I couldn't tell you. But ask me about George Clooney and I can rattle off facts faster than a machine gun."

They both laughed. Gemma felt a sweetness filter through her system.

They continued down the shoreline in perfect, contented silence. Gemma pondered the lonesome cry of the gulls as they wheeled overhead, their movements looking almost choreographed. She inhaled deeply; the salt tang in the crisp fall air had a revivifying effect.

"You grew up near here?"

Sean nodded. "About ten minutes away."

"How wonderful, to be able to go to the beach anytime you wanted."

"It was pretty great, I won't lie." His arm stole around her shoulders. "You said you have relatives here on Long Island?"

"My cousin Paul in Commack. Everyone else is still in Brooklyn."

"Yeah, I meant to ask you about that." His expression was curious. "How come you didn't talk to your mom at the christening party?"

Gemma felt a small quickening in her chest. "I'm surprised you noticed."

"I noticed everything about you that day."

"I'm flattered." She felt safe with his arm around her—

safe enough to talk about what was, for her, a very painful subject. "My mom and I don't get along. I'm an only child, and I guess I've failed to live up to her expectations."

"How? You're smart; you run your own business."

"In my mom's eyes I'm just plain weird."

"What did she expect from you?" He sounded indignant.

"A mother-daughter house in Bensonhurst and at least three grandchildren. So far I've failed to deliver."

Sean stopped, drawing her into his arms. "She's crazy," he murmured, pushing her wind-whipped hair from her face. "You're perfect just the way you are."

He lowered his head, lips meeting hers perfectly. His tongue playfully danced along her lips, and then it was inside her mouth, blood pounding in Gemma's ears as Sean crushed her to him. *Thank you for this man,* she thought. *I never thought I could be so lucky.*

"Ever make love on a beach?" Gemma whispered slyly.

Sean drew back. "It's the middle of the day!"

"I'm not talking about now! I'm talking sometime."

He kissed her forehead. "Someday. I promise." He took her hand and they resumed walking along the shore. Then Sean stopped. "Wait—have *you* ever made love on a beach?"

Gemma grinned mischievously. "You really want to go down that road?"

"Nope. Besides, there's no need to. I'm the first and only man you've ever been with. The end."

Gemma laughed and they ambled on in silence for a few minutes more. She loved that they could just be quiet together.

"Do you get along with your folks?" she finally asked.

"Yeah," Sean said without hesitation. "I'm a lot like my dad—a chip off the old adrenaline junkie block."

"Really?"

"Oh, yeah. Most firefighters are adrenaline junkies, not

that they'll admit it. There's a certain feeling you get when
you climb on the truck and head off to a situation where
you don't know exactly what's waiting for you. It's a total
rush."

"And what if what's waiting for you is a life-and-death
situation?"

Sean shrugged. "You deal with it."

"Isn't it scary?"

Sean kicked up a spray of sand. "Sometimes. Usually
there isn't enough time to think about it."

Gemma swallowed nervously. The thought of him rushing into burning buildings—of saying goodbye to him before he left for work and the possibility that he might not
come home again—overwhelmed her. Just picturing it
made her feel queasy. She pushed it from her mind. Far off
in the distance, a gray cloud stole onto the horizon, mar-
ring the azure perfection of the sky. Gemma clutched
Sean's hand and pressed it to her lips. She hoped it wasn't
an omen.

"I have an idea."

Gemma's ears perked up as she watched Sean at the
stove, flipping pancakes. Last night, he'd made her a deli-
cious portobello mushroom quiche and salad, followed by
the most exquisite Scottish shortbread she'd ever tasted.
They'd spent the evening relaxing, reading, and making
love. Gemma thought that if she could fall asleep to the
soothing, steady rhythm of the waves every night, she'd
never suffer insomnia again. Of course, having Sean's
body to spoon with and keep her warm hadn't hurt either.

Wrapping her robe tighter against the ocean chill, she
approached him. "What's that?"

"How about we pop over to my folks' house this afternoon and say hi?"

"Your folks?" *Meet his parents? Now? So soon?*

"Yeah. Sunday's the day my mom makes a big roast and my sisters and their families come over. I think it would be fun."

Gemma didn't quite know what to say. She was flattered Sean thought her "family worthy." It meant he thought their relationship had real potential.

Sean looked bemused as he slid two more perfectly done pancakes on a plate and poured more batter on the grill. "What? Are you nervous?"

"Of course! I want to make a good impression."

He ruffled her hair, kissing the top of her head. "You will."

Gemma's mind went into overdrive. "Is there a florist around here? Should I bring flowers? I can't show up empty-handed."

"Relax! Yes, there's a florist. We'll stop off before we go to my folks." Hope flickered in his eyes. "Is that a yes, then?"

"Yes, yes, yes!" Gemma chirped happily. "I'd love to meet your family."

Sean's family lived two towns over in Oceanside. Gemma was so nervous she couldn't speak on the short drive over. Instead, she contented herself with looking out the window, taking in the scenery, and trying to imagine what it was like for Sean to grow up here.

"This is it," Sean announced after a few minutes, turning onto a leafy cul-de-sac. Gemma watched as Sean waved to a man washing his Lexus in the driveway; the man squinted to recognize Sean, then waved back. Sean slowed in front of a split-level with maroon shutters and white trim. The driveway was filled with three minivans. One had an image of the Twin Towers painted on the rear window, and beneath it the words FDNY FINAL CALL/9-11-01/FOREVER IN OUR HEARTS."

He hustled around to the passenger side and opened the door for Gemma, who could feel her heart beginning to race as they started toward the Kennealy house.

"Nervous?"

"A little," Gemma admitted, grateful for his concern.

"It'll be a cakewalk, I swear." They walked up the front steps. "Just two things," he added, pressing the doorbell.

"What's that?"

"Don't get Tom started on the Jets."

"And—?"

There was the sound of a lock being clicked back.

"Don't say anything about being a witch."

CHAPTER

08

Sitting in the Kennealys' crowded living room, Gemma struggled to keep Sean's family straight. There were his parents, who insisted she call them Mary and Steve. There was Sean's sister Christine and her husband—Joe? Joel? Gemma wasn't sure she'd heard his name correctly, and was too embarrassed to ask him to repeat it.

Christine and Joe/Joel seemed to be the parents of three little girls, the youngest an infant. Or did the baby belong to his sister Pat and her husband, Tom? No, wait: Tom made a crack over dinner about both his *boys* becoming firefighters. That meant Pat and Tom were the parents of the twins. That left Sean's sister Megan and her new boyfriend, Jason. Luckily, Jason seemed as overwhelmed as Gemma, and she was glad he was there. It meant she wouldn't be the only one put under the family microscope at day's end.

"More coffee, Gemma?" Like Stavros, Sean's mom seemed to have the coffeepot permanently welded to her hand.

Gemma held up her mug. "I would love some Mrs. . . . Mary."

"Here you go." She topped Gemma off, moving in a graceful arc around the room, providing refills. Gemma contrasted Mary's easygoing nature with that of her own mother, who would go into full-blown cardiac arrest if anyone dared bring food or drink into her living room. In fact, she cordoned the room off with a velvet rope as if it were a museum.

Don't say anything about being a witch. He couldn't have shocked her more if he'd turned to her and declared he had superpowers. What did he think she was going to do? Pull down her jeans and moon them all with her tattoo? She knew when it was appropriate to be open about it, and when it wasn't! Meeting a boyfriend's family for the first time fell into the latter category.

"Gemma, would you mind helping me with the dishes in the kitchen?"

Gemma smiled affably and rose, following Mrs. Kennealy and Megan. She was pleased to be included, though she knew part of the reason she was being spirited away was so they could quiz her about Sean. How many family secrets and stories had women swapped in the kitchen under the auspices of doing chores?

A system was quickly established: Mrs. Kennealy scraped food off the plates into the garbage. Gemma rinsed them, and Megan loaded them in the dishwasher.

"So," Mrs. Kennealy began, and Gemma held her breath. *Here it comes.* "How long have you known Sean?"

"A few months. We live in the same building."

"And you run your own store in the city, you said?" Sean's mother was looking at Gemma with interest.

Gemma nodded. "Yes. I sell books, candles, incense, that sort of thing."

"Cool," chimed Megan, who at twenty was the baby of the family.

"Sounds interesting," Mrs. Kennealy agreed.

Megan looked up from where she was bent over the lower rack of the dishwasher. "Has he dragged you to a stupid firehouse party yet?"

"Megan." Mrs. Kennealy flashed her a look of warning before smiling warmly at Gemma. "For some reason, my youngest daughter has a problem with firefighters, despite the fact half the men she knows do it for a living."

"Maybe that's why," Megan sniffed derisively. "It's like a cult. Get out now while you can."

Gemma grabbed another plate and ran it under the tap. "What don't you like about it?"

"Megan." Mrs. Kennealy's voice was a warning.

"Ma, she asked me!" Megan whined.

"Fine," said Mrs. Kennealy with a long-suffering sigh. "Give her your little speech."

Megan smirked triumphantly. " 'Why I Will Never Go Out with a Fireman,' by Megan Kennealy. One: They drink too much."

Mrs. Kennealy glared with indignation. "That's a stereotype and you know it!"

Megan ignored her. "Two: They work fucked-up hours. Three: For what they do, the pay is absolute shit."

"Nice language," said her mother.

"Four: Over half of all firefighter marriages end in divorce. Why? Because five: Firefighters are about as open with their emotions as the Sphinx. And they drink. And the pay is shit so they have to work lots of overtime or second jobs to make money, so they don't see their families." Her voice dripped with sarcasm. "Oh! Did I forget to mention the pay is shit?"

Mrs. Kennealy's frown returned. "They don't do it for the pay."

"Oh, that's right, they do it to serve, I forgot. Which brings me to six: I don't want to hitch my wagon to anyone who might die on me when he goes to work." She smiled at Gemma gaily. "That about covers it."

"Very nice," Mrs. Kennealy said sourly. "I'm sure Sean will want to thank you for sharing your views with his new girlfriend—views which are immature, I might add." She glanced up at Gemma apologetically from the plate she was scraping. "Megan prides herself on saying outrageous things just to get a reaction. Don't pay any attention."

"It's all right," Gemma assured her. She winked at Megan covertly to let her know she wasn't siding with Sean's mother, but inside, Megan's words had made her uneasy. "One thing Megan said did interest me," she timidly admitted aloud.

"What's that?"

"Well, how do you deal with the danger factor?"

Mrs. Kennealy blinked. "You just do."

"But how?" She hoped Mrs. Kennealy didn't think her too pushy, but this was preying heavily on her mind. If she and Sean were truly going to be a couple, she was going to have to deal with the harsh realities of his job.

"Sean's father and I had a rule: Never go to bed mad at one another. That advice holds whether you're married to a firefighter or not. Beyond that, the only advice I can give is if he wants to talk, listen, and if he doesn't, leave him be. The truth is, some women can't deal with it. The uncertainty drives them crazy."

"So does the macho bullshit," Megan added under her breath. "And the stress. And—"

Mrs. Kennealy spun angrily to face her daughter. "One more word out of you and you can find someone else to pay your college tuition, got that?"

"Fine." Megan sulked.

Their dynamic made Gemma uncomfortable, reminding her of her own relationship with her mother at that age, the two of them constantly locking horns. Yet on another level, it felt completely normal. Dante-esque. She wondered if they sparred like this in front of everyone. If not, then it had to mean they felt comfortable around her. She felt accepted.

From out in the living room came the sound of roaring laughter. Megan rolled her eyes. "Some stupid firehouse story, I'm sure. They've got a million."

"For once she's not exaggerating," Mrs. Kennealy added with a rueful shake of the head. "They should write a book." Her eyes strayed to the clock above the sink. "I hope Uncle Jack and Aunt Bridie get here soon. I'm dying for a piece of that chocolate cake."

"So, have a piece," Megan urged. "You made it. You've earned the right to nibble."

Mrs. Kennealy frowned with disapproval. "That wouldn't be polite. And we don't want our guests thinking we're shanty, do we?"

Gemma blinked, confused. "Shanty?"

"Shanty Irish, as opposed to lace curtain."

Gemma stared blankly.

Mrs. Kennealy looked surprised. "You've never heard that expression?"

"No."

"It's an old, rude way of saying high-class Irish versus low-class Irish."

"We're definitely low-class," Megan joked.

"Speak for yourself," her mother said. She bit her lip, restive, unable to tear her gaze from the cake sitting on the counter. "Maybe I will have a piece. I'm sure the O'Sheas won't mind."

"*You were kind* of quiet during dessert," said Sean when they got back to the Long Beach apartment.

"I was thinking about some things your sister said to me in the kitchen," Gemma said, unbuttoning her shirt.

Sean didn't respond immediately, choosing instead to

perch on the edge of the bed to remove his socks. When he spoke, his voice had an edge. "Let me guess: She gave you her 'Why Firefighters Suck' speech."

"Yup." Gemma moved to the closet to hang up her blouse. "Why is she so vehement?" she asked over her shoulder.

Sean's eyes followed her. "Well, for one thing, she knows it's going to get up my mother's nose. And if there's one thing Megan enjoys, it's trying to raise Mom's blood pressure."

"Ah, yes, parent baiting," Gemma mused as she slipped out of her yoga pants. "One of the pleasures of being twenty."

Sean chuckled in agreement. "The other reason she's so pissy is that she was dating a probie last year. They met at a St. Patrick's Day Dance at the Knights of Columbus Hall in Mineola, I think it was." Sean looked tired. "Anyway, they were going all hot and heavy and pfftt! One day he just pulls the plug, no explanation, nothing. She's still not over it. Her way of dealing with it is to vil-lify all of us."

"Poor Megan."

"Yeah, it was a pretty raw deal." Sean rose to unzip his jeans. "I think she's pissed my dad wasn't around a lot, too. By the time she came along, he was doing a lot of carpen-try work on the side to keep our heads above water."

"I see." So Megan wasn't exaggerating. The uneasiness Gemma felt in the Kennealys' kitchen returned.

"You and my mom seemed to get along okay," Sean ob-served as he slithered out of his pants, standing there in just his briefs.

"She's nice," Gemma replied with a smile as she unfas-tened her bra and put it to rest on the dresser. "She made me feel very welcome."

Sean moved to the sliding glass doors looking out on the ocean. "When you were in the bathroom, she asked me what perfume you were wearing. Said it reminded her of the sixties."

Gemma slipped on the oversized T-shirt she intended to sleep in, then joined him at the doors. "Is that good or bad?"

"Good, I think."

"I hope."

Moving behind her, Sean wrapped his arms around her, pulling her close. "Did you have fun today?"

Gemma's eyes drifted shut. "Yes and no."

Sean lifted her hair, pressing his mouth against her right ear. "I'm listening."

"I was a little upset when you told me not to mention being a witch." She turned around in his arms. Some things had to be said face-to-face, though God knows, she wished they could have this entire conversation looking out at the dark ocean.

"Gemma—"

"Let me finish."

Sean dipped his head, acquiescent.

"You made me feel dumb, Sean. Of course I wasn't going to mention it! Not the first time I met them! But it does make me wonder . . ." She hesitated.

Sean pushed a stray lock of hair behind her ear. "What?"

"If it embarrasses you in some way."

"Of course it doesn't," he scoffed.

"Because eventually they're going to find out."

"I know that. But not yet." There was mild panic in his voice.

"When?" she asked softly, running a finger up and down his bare shoulder.

"When it's time." He drew her into a more intimate embrace. "Enough talking." He pressed his lips to hers.

"Trying to hush me up with kisses, huh?" Gemma teased.

"You object?"

Gemma laughed, wrapping her arms around his neck. She assumed Sean was strong, but she wasn't prepared for him to lift her with one arm and throw her over his shoulder like some modern-day caveman.

"What are you doing?" she cried, watching the sliding glass doors recede as he carried her to the bed. As swiftly as he'd picked her up, that's how delicately he put her down, the nubby chenille of the bedspread a soft shock against her skin. Then he was on her, skin sliding against burning skin, lips demanding and hard as he greedily pressed his mouth to her throat. Gemma moaned as the twin torments of heat and desire coiled themselves around the two of them, binding them. She couldn't tell where Sean left and she began. There was only this moment, this outpouring of need that seemed unstoppable.

Sean lifted his head just enough to look into her eyes. "Kiss me," he demanded.

Breathless, Gemma did as she was told, powerless to do anything else. She lifted her head off the bed slightly and, gripping his head in her hands, pulled his face down to hers and held it there, one second, two seconds, three, their lips almost touching but not quite, their heated breath mingling. Unable to take it any longer, Sean gave a guttural groan and pressed his mouth to hers, raw and desperate. The taste of him, Gemma thought dizzily, was like wine, like divinity. She clutched him close, afraid that if she loosened her grip, he would turn to an apparition and disappear into the night without a trace. She wanted every nerve in her body to register that this was a real, solid, flesh-and-blood man who was pressing into her with all his might. A real, solid man who wanted her.

Two pulses were fluttering wildly within her now: the one at the base of her throat, throbbing like a trapped, quivering bird, and the one pounding between her legs. Squirming in desperation beneath him, she hooked her thumbs in the waistband of his briefs and tugged. The motion seemed to inflame Sean: Without a sound he rose up and tore the briefs from his hips before crashing back down onto her, his hard-on burning against her. Gemma wondered if he could tell how badly she wanted him as she pressed herself urgently against him. She would not be complete until he had filled her. She would not rest until they spoke the same blazing language of the soul.

Ravenous. That was the word that sprang to Gemma's mind as Sean's mouth raced over her upper torso, tongue pausing to tease at her nipples through the cotton of her T-shirt. Thought ceased, veering into pure sensation. *Hot, wet, burning, yes*—Gemma's overloaded mind could barely form the words. *Rough, hard, shocking, please.* She knew she should be patient, knew how it all would end and that it would be good, so damn good, but she couldn't help herself. The conflagration burning within her was out of control. She needed relief now.

Sean knew. Gemma sensed he was just waiting for her to give him a signal. And so, too overcome to speak, she dragged her nails across his back. She lapped at him like a cat. Sean reared up and, in a move both unexpected and thrilling, roughly parted her legs, plunging his fingers deep within her. The room reverberated with the sound of Gemma's shocked screams, so loud they drowned out the background music of the surf. His pacing perfect, the thumb of his free hand caressed her sex, coaxing her to delirium while his nimble fingers dipped and played. Trembling, eager, she let herself plunge into the shuddering abyss, knowing that Sean would be there to catch her when she broke free of the bounds of earth. She was tumbling, flying, eternal. She was perfectly, absolutely his.

Weak, she opened her eyes, whispering her thanks. Smiling, Sean kissed her sweating forehead before gently withdrawing his hand. Gemma knew what was going to happen next; she craved it, body already retensing in an-

ticipation. She swooned as his fingers grasped her hips
tightly in preparation. And then he was inside her, burning,
moving, demanding, each punch of his hips against hers an
invitation. *Come . . . with . . . me.* Gemma's heart danced
madly in her chest. Come with him? Gladly. Tightening
herself around him, she answered his invitation.

He loved that. Loved it. Gemma could tell by the frenzy
of his body, his driving need pushing both of them farther
and farther up the bed. Reaching up, she curled her fingers
around the wooden spindles of the headboard, bracing herself. And then it came: the breaking of the dam as he
poured himself into her, breathing her name. *Gemma.
Gemma. Gemma.* Was it possible to get drunk on the sound
of one's own name? If so, then she was plastered, she was
destroyed, she would never, never move again. Above her,
Sean's body still quivered in the aftermath of their fierce
union. Gemma slowly lowered her hands from the headboard and wrapped them around Sean's back. They were
both limp, wrecked.

And more satisfied than words could ever express.

Afterward, lying in Sean's arms, Gemma realized that
bed was where they communicated best. It was just the two
of them, reading each other perfectly. No crossed wires, no
fears on her part about what she might be getting herself
into, no fears on his about what she believed. They simply
were.

Lifting her head from Sean's chest, she looked at him.
"You awake?" she whispered.

"Uh-huh." The arm he had clasped around her tickled
her shoulder. "What's up?" he asked drowsily.

"Nothing." She put her head down to rest again on his
chest. *Except I'm falling in love with you.*

The realization scared her since she had no idea if he
felt the same. He obviously felt something—he'd taken her

to meet his family and had just made voracious love to her. But was it *love?* Were men and women speaking of the same emotion when they used that word? A shaft of moonlight dissected the bed with its diagonal glow. Outside, Gemma could hear the wind coming off the ocean, buffeting the sliding glass doors, which trembled slightly in their tracks.

"I think there's going to be a storm," she murmured.

"Mmm." Sean drew her closer. "Go to sleep now."

Gemma snuggled close to him, enjoying every second as their legs twined together beneath the tangle of covers. She sighed, planting a series of tiny kisses on his chest before closing her eyes.

Everything was going to be all right.

CHAPTER 09

"*Where were you* this weekend?" Michael asked as he strolled through the door of the Golden Bough.

"Away," Gemma answered with a secretive smile, moving over to make room for him behind the counter.

"With Sean?"

"Sean who?" Gemma asked as she put on a Clannad CD.

"I know all about you and Firefighter Joe."

"You told him I liked bagpipes, didn't you?"

Michael's face lit up. "Did I do good?"

"Very good."

"Of course, I could have told him the truth."

"What's that?"

"That your idea of a good time is dissecting old episodes of 'Charmed,' but I held back."

"I appreciate that, Mikey. Truly."

"Anything for my favorite cousin. Did you have a good time?"

"Yes." Gemma slid back onto her stool. "We were in

Long Beach. A friend of Sean's owns an apartment there and he lets Sean use it sometimes."

"Sweet."

"It was."

"You really like this guy?"

"I do, but . . ."

Michael scowled. "But what?"

Gemma stared down at her lap. "I don't know. The whole firefighter thing makes me nervous."

"What, the fact he could burn to a crisp on any given day?"

Gemma jerked her head up, shocked.

"That *is* what's got you spooked, right?"

"Kinda," Gemma mumbled. "That and some other things. I'm not so sure we fit, you know?"

"Gee, why not?" Michael replied sarcastically. "Just because you're an Italian witch who runs an occult shop and he's a fireman who thinks a dive like O'Toole's is a good place for a first date? Sounds like you two have a ton in common to me."

Gemma cocked her head appraisingly. "I'm trying to remember: Were you always an ass, or did you gradually become one over time?"

"Came out of the womb with ASS stamped across my forehead, *cara*. Sorry." He leaned back to turn the music down a notch. "My advice? Just go with the flow and see what happens."

Gemma couldn't resist a smirk. "You mean the way you did with Theresa, Mr. Read My Tarot Cards or I'll Die?"

Michael colored. "That was different. That was fate."

Gemma burst out laughing. "Oh, I see. And this isn't. Michael Dante, the grand vizier of romantic relationships."

"I'm just saying," Michael huffed.

"I know what you're saying, and I appreciate it."

"Is he good to you?"

The way he said it, with the barest hint of a threat as if

he were Gemma's older, protective brother, brought a smile to her face. "He's wonderful, Michael. Don't worry."

Michael rubbed her back. "You're my favorite cousin, Gem. Of course I worry."

"Don't. I can take care of myself."

"Yeah, well, I'm not so sure Nonna can." He looked pained. "That's why I'm here."

Gemma felt a wave of anxiety. "What's going on?"

"A couple of weeks ago, Anthony and Angie took Nonna to church at her usual time. Angie decided to stay. She told Ant that ten minutes into Mass, Nonna got up and started wandering around. At first Angie thought she just couldn't remember where the bathroom was. But when she went to get her, Nonna didn't seem to know where she was, or who Angie was, for that matter."

Gemma tensed.

"Then, on Thursday night, Nonna ran a bath for herself and left the taps on. The tub overflowed, and water started dripping through the ceiling."

Gemma wound her fingers together tightly.

"You should see the water damage. When the ceiling started leaking, Nonna panicked and called me. By the time I got there, the ceiling was starting to bow. I turned off the taps, and cut a hole in the kitchen ceiling so that it wouldn't collapse. You wouldn't believe the friggin' deluge. I said, 'Nonna, what the hell were you thinking?' I swear to God, Gem, she looked like a scared little kid who was afraid of getting in trouble. 'I don't remember turning the water on,' she said."

"Shit." A million thoughts ran through Gemma's mind, none of them positive.

Michael's gaze was quizzical. "Has she seemed forgetful with you? Different? Absentminded?"

"She has seemed forgetful. But it could just be old age."

"It could be," said Michael, not sounding convinced.

A sense of foreboding seemed to swirl through the

store, oppressive and heavy. Gemma could barely look at Michael without her chest beginning to constrict. "You're afraid it's more serious, aren't you?" she asked.

"Yeah." Michael looked up, eyes misty.

Gemma clutched at hope. "It could be a million things, Mikey. Drug interactions. Lots of old people go to different doctors and they don't tell one what the other has prescribed."

"It's not her drugs. I took her to the doctor and I brought the list of her prescriptions with me. None of them interact."

"Maybe we should get her to a specialist?"

"We are." Michael was grim. "Theresa's getting the names and numbers of top gerontologists in the city. Once she does, we'll make some appointments."

"That could take months."

"Not if your husband plays for the Blades and can get the doctor rink-side tickets to a home game," Michael explained matter-of-factly.

Gemma reached out, squeezing Michael's shoulder. "We'll figure this out. You know we will." Her mind continued racing to come up with explanations for her grandmother's memory lapses. Hardening of the arteries. Lack of sleep. Lots of old people had trouble sleeping. Maybe Nonna wasn't sleeping and that's why she was forgetful.

"Depending on what the doctors say, we'll have a family meeting and figure out what to do."

"Who's taking her to the doctor?"

Michael glanced away. "Your mother and Aunt Millie."

"What?" Gemma squawked.

"She's their mother, Gemma."

"One of us should go, too. You or me or Ant or Angie or Theresa. Don't you think?"

Michael looked troubled. "They'll think we think they're incompetent if we suggest it."

"They are incompetent!" Gemma cried. She could just

picture it: her mother tapping her foot impatiently, barely listening to what the doctor said because she was dying to get out of there and make it home in time for *Oprah,* while beside her, Millie the Sicilian chimney twitched with nicotine withdrawal.

"Gem." Michael's voice was gentle. "One of us can always call to speak with the doctor afterwards."

But Gemma was adamant. "I'm going, Michael. To hell with hurting my mother's feelings. This is Nonna we're talking about here. *Nonna.* No way am I going to rely on Heckle and Jeckle to come back and give us a report. You and Theresa call me when the appointment's made and I'll go with my mother and Millie."

"Okay," said Michael, sounding dubious. He checked his watch and stood. "I hate to depress and run, but I've got to get to Met Gar." He rustled Gemma's sleeve. "You gonna be okay, chooch?"

"Yes. You?"

Michael nodded, wrapping his arms around her in a big bear hug. "As soon as Theresa gets an appointment, I'll call you. Meantime, try not to worry."

But that was easier said than done. Gemma decided to visit her grandmother.

Ever since she was little, Gemma loved the smell of Nonna's house. It smelled fresh, as if her grandmother had just finished spring cleaning right before you visited. It wasn't until she was older that Gemma realized the scent permeating Nonna's home was rosemary. Nonna grew it in pots around the house as well as outside in her postage stamp–sized yard. Gemma loved to sit on the front stoop on summer evenings and wait for a passing breeze to help envelop her in its scent. Even now, no matter where she was, the smell of rosemary always brought her straight back to her childhood, and to happy times spent in Bensonhurst with the woman who made her feel special.

Gemma phoned ahead of time to let Nonna know she'd be stopping by the next evening. Even so, Nonna's face creased with surprise as she swung open the front door.

"*Bella!* I wish you'd told me you were coming, I'd have bought some biscotti!"

Gemma's heart sank. "I did tell you, Nonna. Last night. On the phone. Remember?"

"Oh, right, right," Nonna said hastily, ushering Gemma inside. Gemma sensed Nonna knew she was starting to forget things but was trying to cover up.

Gemma held up a paper bag. "I brought the biscotti, so you don't have to worry."

"*Perfetto!*" Nonna clasped her gnarled hands together in delight. "Come, we'll make some espresso, yes?"

"Okay." Gemma wasn't sure her nervous system, only recently introduced to the world of caffeine, would be able to handle Nonna's espresso. The family joke was that it could be used to tar roofs in an emergency. Screw it. One cup of espresso was not going to kill her.

Following her grandmother into the kitchen, she was shocked by the sight of the sagging, water-stained ceiling.

"Have you called Mr. Rosetti yet?" Gemma asked, referring to the sheet rock contractor whom her father had known for years. "You really need to get the ceiling replaced as soon as possible, Nonna."

Nonna glanced up at the ceiling. "I will, I will. Everything in its time." She fluttered her hands at Gemma. "Sit, sit."

Gemma sat, carefully watching her grandmother prepare the espresso. Her movements were as steady and sure as ever. She knew where the coffee was kept, she measured out the right amount, she knew how to turn the machine on. So far, so good.

"So, *bella*," Nonna said as she arranged the biscotti on a plate, "tell me what's new and exciting."

"Nothing. Well, something," Gemma amended. "Someone."

Nonna's eyes lit up. "Yes?"

"His name is Sean Kennealy. He's a firefighter."

Nonna's face fell. "Irish?"

"Yeess," Gemma chastised, half rising from her chair in case Nonna needed help getting into hers. But she was fine.

Nonna sighed. "I guess it's too much to hope for that you would find an Italian boy."

"What's wrong with an Irish boy?"

Nonna's tiny, gnarled fingers curled around a piece of biscotti. "They drink too much."

Gemma frowned, disappointed. "Not true and you know it."

Nonna bit down on her cookie. "I know what I know."

"In this case you're wrong."

"So, this Irish boy." Gemma loved that her grandmother referred to a thirty-five-year-old man as a "boy." "Are you making sex with him?"

"Nonna!" Gemma couldn't believe her grandmother would say such a thing.

"That's all men want, the sex," Nonna groused. "You tell them no, they say yes. Poking, poking, poking until you give way."

Gemma stared at her grandmother in disbelief. Who was this woman sitting across the table from her? She had never heard Nonna talk this way. Never. She knew her grandmother was devilish and irreverent, but this was something different. Correction: This was someone different.

"Nonna," Gemma repeated, her voice gentler this time. "Are you feeling all right?"

"I'm feeling fine," Nonna snapped. "Why?"

"Nothing, you're just talking strange, is all."

"Nothing strange about the truth, *cara.*"

Perhaps it was cruel, but Gemma decided to conduct a little test. "What happened to the ceiling, Nonna?"

Ignoring her, Nonna rose from the table to check the espresso machine.

"Nonna?"

"Someone left the water running," Nonna mumbled. "That's what Michael says."

"Someone?"

Nonna was silent.

Gemma rose and put her arms around her grandmother. "You don't remember, do you, Non? You don't remember leaving the taps on."

"No," Nonna whispered. Her expression was desperate. "But don't tell. Don't tell."

"I won't tell," Gemma promised, steering her grandmother back to the table. "Here, you sit. I'll get the espresso."

"I keep forgetting things. But I don't remember forgetting. Maybe I'm *ubatz.* Who knows?"

"You're not crazy."

"Then why else—?"

"I don't know," Gemma said, preparing the espresso. "But we're going to find out." She turned around to check her grandmother's expression, surprised to see the suspicion in her eyes.

"Who's we?" Nonna demanded.

"Me, mom, and Aunt Millie. We're going to take you to a special doctor and we're going to get to the bottom of what's wrong."

"I'll tell you what's wrong," Nonna said, huffing. "Your mother comes creeping around here every day, poking, prying, asking questions. She thinks I don't know she steals my tomatoes, either. She should mind her own business, that one. And Millie! I should have drowned that one at birth. Her and Betty Anne."

Gemma flinched. Some alien had possessed her grandmother. That was all there was to it.

"Don't say things like that," Gemma admonished. "It's not nice."

"I'm old. I don't have to be nice."

Gemma laughed. Now that sounded like her grandmother. Maybe all wasn't lost.

Nonna took a sip of espresso, declaring it splendid. Gemma did the same and almost passed the black sludge through her nose. It was beyond horrible: It was toxic. Her first sip would be her last.

"Do you want to hear more about my boyfriend?" Gemma asked, trying to get off the topic of her mother and her two aunts, who apparently were lucky to have survived infancy.

"Sure," Nonna said eagerly. "I want to hear every blessed detail."

Gemma told her as much as she deemed necessary and flattering.

"Does he know about *La Stregheria?*" Nonna asked.

Gemma nodded.

"And—?"

"He's a little confused by it," Gemma admitted.

"Confused you can work with. Fear you can't." Nonna reached across the table for Gemma's hand. As always, Gemma was shocked by how cold it was. Cold but soft, the sweet scent of Jergen's lotion wafting up to her nostrils. Gemma loved that scent. Almond. It was Nonna's scent.

"This is what I'm going to do," Nonna said, squeezing Gemma's hand. "I'm going to light a candle for you at St. Finbar's on Sunday, and pray to the BVM that all your dreams come true."

Gemma was touched. "Thank you."

"And then," Nonna mumbled, turning away as she rose to get a refill of espresso, "I'm going to say a special prayer to the *querciola* for you."

Gemma leaned forward, straining to hear. "What did you just say?"

Nonna looked confused. "What?"

"Just now. Who did you say you would pray to?"

Nonna looked thoughtful. Then her expression faded into one of blankness. She shook her head slowly. "I don't remember."

Gemma let it go. But the word—*querciola*—stuck in her mind. It sounded familiar, but she couldn't quite place it. She'd have to poke around, do some research when she got home.

"*That was Peter* Gabriel with 'Shock the Monkey.' Before that, Elvis Costello told us to 'Pump It Up'—Yes, sir!—and we started the set with a classic from AC/DC, 'You Shook Me All Night Long.' Stay tuned, weather coming at ya in just five minutes."

Going to commercial, Frankie whipped off her headphones and stared at Gemma in disbelief. "Excuse me, what did you just say?"

"I think my grandmother might be a witch."

Frankie looked doubtful as she hopped off her chair to load a stack of CDs back in their cases. It was Saturday afternoon, and she was filling in for another jock. It felt odd to Gemma to see her in the studio in the daytime.

"I told her about Sean, right? And in addition to telling me she'd say a prayer to the BVM—"

"Who?"

"It's Catholic shorthand for the Blessed Virgin Mary: BVM."

"Sounds like a terrorist group, but go on."

"She mumbled something about saying a special prayer to the *querciola*. So I looked it up. According to one of my books on Italian witchcraft, the *querciola* are special spirits who look out for lovers."

"Gemma, no way is your grandmother a witch. The woman practically lives at St. Finbar's."

"Maybe she's both."

"Wouldn't that qualify as a 'Pass Go, Proceed Directly to Hell'–type situation?"

"How else would you explain it, then?"

"She's old and she was born in Italy, right?" Frankie trekked across the worn carpet of the studio and began putting CDs away. "It's probably something she heard about when she was a child, some old superstition." Gemma frowned. "C'mon, Gem, think about it. Your grandmother's house has more religious imagery per square inch than the Vatican."

"True." She shrugged. "I just thought it was interesting, that's all."

Her eyes followed Frankie as she hustled back to the control board, pressing a button that launched into another commercial. She loved watching Frankie at work—she had impeccable timing honed after years of practice, not to mention between-song patter she made look effortless. Frankie was in her element in the studio.

"I see you're not wearing your hat," said Gemma.

"Nope."

"The baldness has cleared up, then?"

"Scoff all you want," Frankie said heatedly, "but my hairline is receding. Just not as badly as I thought."

"And the sunglasses? Are you hung over?"

"No."

"What's the deal, then?"

"I think I'm developing cataracts." She slipped her headphones back on. Gemma held still while the ON AIR sign above the studio door lit up. "It's fifty-five degrees and sunny in Midtown Manhattan on this glorious Saturday afternoon. Don't know about you, but I can't think of a better way to celebrate the day than with a little taste o' the Fabs." Frankie hit a button and the opening chords of

"Good Day Sunshine" filled the studio. She turned to Gemma. "Go ahead and laugh. Accuse me of being a hypochondriac."

"I didn't say anything!"

"You didn't have to." Frankie lowered the sunglasses, squinting. "Bright lights hurt my eyes. That's one of the symptoms."

"You know, God forbid you ever do have anything seriously wrong with you. No one will believe you."

Frankie stuck out her tongue before pushing the glasses back up her nose and turning to a nearby computer. "What did your grandmother have to say about Sean?" she asked, typing.

"What do you think? She's disappointed he's not Italian."

"Have you met his firefighting buddies yet?"

"No."

"I'm surprised. I always thought firefighters thought of their comrades as their second family."

The observation pricked at Gemma. She'd met his flesh-and-blood family. Didn't that count?

"*You* still haven't met Sean."

"Correction: Sean hasn't met *me*. Let's not get confused over who's more important here."

Gemma chuckled. "True." She took a sip of the tea she'd brought with her in a thermos. "Think I should say something? About meeting his friends?"

"Absolutely." Frankie turned to her. "And find out if he has any single friends while you're at it."

"You serious?"

"I wouldn't mind putting an end to my dating drought."

"Hhmm." In all honesty, Gemma couldn't imagine Frankie with a firefighter. She tended to be attracted to more flamboyant types: musicians, foreign jugglers, performance artists who smeared their body with crude oil to protest foreign cartels, that type of thing. The more offbeat the man, the more intrigued Frankie was. And that's when it hit her.

"I think I might know someone!"

Frankie's eyes lit up. "Who?"

"The guy I've been giving tarot lessons to. Uther."

"The one you said looks like a refugee from ZZ Top?"

"Yes, but he's really nice, Frankie. Really smart. He has a photographic memory. And"—she wasn't sure if this would be an enticement, but it was worth a try—"he makes a boatload of money."

Frankie grunted. "Huh. I'll think about it. In the meantime you need to think about meeting Sean's friends."

"What are you doing still up?"

Gemma sat curled on Sean's couch, sipping peppermint tea. It was 6 A.M. Sunday morning, and Sean was just returning from covering another firefighter's shift. There was more than surprise in his eyes when he saw her. There was dismay.

Gemma's gaze danced away. "I couldn't sleep."

"Oh, honey." Sean sat beside her and wrapped an arm around her. "You've got to do something about this. This is crazy."

They'd been together two months now, and rather than getting used to his being a firefighter, her anxiety seemed to be getting worse. She did protection spells, but nothing seemed to quell her nerves. She was okay when she was at the store, because work gave her something to focus on. But the rest of the time, she was haunted by the sound of sirens. When a fire truck roared down the street, her heart stopped as she worried about where the men inside it were going, if they had families, if they'd all return safely. Night shifts, like the one Sean had just pulled, were the worst. She would lie awake staring at the ceiling, wondering

the kiss he'd given her before he'd walked out the door
would be the last one they'd ever share.

"Did you get any sleep at all?"

Embarassed, Gemma shook her head. He was near
enough that she could catch his scent: fresh lemon. That
meant he'd showered at the firehouse. Showering at the
firehouse meant he'd gone out to a fire. Maybe more than
one.

"How was work?" she asked quietly, knowing she'd get
the same answer she always did. Sean didn't know it, but
his tendency toward being tight lipped contributed to her
anxiety as well. She was a Dante, for God's sake. She was
used to dealing with people who called each other up to
announce they'd just blown their nose.

Sean yawned, seeming to consider her question. "It was
okay. Slow."

"Any calls?"

Sean rubbed his eyes. "Yeah. One." His bloodshot eyes
met hers. "It was pretty bad. I really don't want to talk
about it, okay?"

Gemma bit at her cuticle anxiously. "Can't you tell me
just a little? I worry so much."

"It was a suicide," Sean said quietly. "Let's leave it at
that."

"Okay." Morbid curiosity roiled inside her but she re-
frained from asking him anything more. The things he saw
in the line of duty were a dual-edged sword. She wanted to
know, but at the same time, she didn't. Better to keep it
light.

"Did the guys like your brownies?"

"Yeah, they were gone in five seconds flat. They inhaled them. Then Ojeda's face swelled up. He's allergic to
walnuts but he scarfed down a bunch anyway."

"Is he okay?"

"He's fine. Leary ran him over to the emergency room
at Lenox Hill. They gave him a shot and sent him on his

merry way." Sean shook his head. "What kind of an idiot forgets he's allergic to walnuts?"

"A hungry one?"

"I'll leave 'em out next time."

"Am I ever going to meet any of these guys? She touched Sean's hand lightly. "They seem to mean a lot to you."

"They do."

"So, let's do something with them and their wives. Or girlfriends. Isn't it about time I met your 'second' family?"

Sean's expression was tentative. "I guess we can figure something out."

"Is everything okay between us?" Gemma asked quietly.

"Why do you ask that?"

"It's just . . ." She paused to find the right words. "We've been dating for two months and I haven't met your friends. Sometimes I get the feeling that you're afraid—"

"You want to meet some of the guys?" Sean cut in, rising from the couch. "Consider it done."

CHAPTER
10

"How do I look?"

Sean looked up from the latest issue of *Firehouse* magazine to see Gemma standing before him in a purple sari, gold bangles ringing her left arm from wrist to elbow. They were going to meet Mike Leary and his wife Ronnie, as well Ted Delaney and his girlfriend Danielle, for dinner at Dante's. At least, that had been the plan. Now Sean wasn't so sure.

"Um . . ."

Gemma twirled for him. "Don't you love it? My friend Kai brought it back for me from India."

Sean scratched his cheek. "It's very—Indian."

Gemma's smile slowly faded. "You don't like it."

"No, no, you look great." She did. She looked exotic, gorgeous, and delectable. To him.

"So—?"

Sean clasped his hands between his knees. "It's a little"—he paused—"it's a little over the top."

"You think so?"

"Yeah, kinda."

Gemma looked surprised. "Oh, well. Guess I'll go change."

Watching her walk back into her bedroom, Sean was wracked with guilt. Who was he to tell her what to wear? The answer came swiftly: the guy who was gonna catch major shit if he showed up at a Brooklyn spaghetti house with Indira Gandhi on his arm. Quirky was one thing. Out-and-out eccentric was another. He wanted his friends to like her, not laugh at her.

"How's this?"

She reappeared in the living room in billowing black pants, beaded Chinese slippers, and a purple velvet tunic with a paisley scarf tossed over one shoulder. Funky but stylish.

"Great," said Sean, meaning it. He crossed to her and took her in his arms, burying his face in her hair. "Aren't you going to wear that perfume I love?"

"I thought it might be over the top."

Their eyes met and Sean saw the imp in hers.

"You busting on me?" he asked, pinching her butt.

"Maybe."

"Wear it," he urged, lightly kissing her temple. "Please."

"Do you think your friends will like me?"

"Of course they will," he assured her—and himself. "What's not to like?"

"Willkommen. Bienvenue. Welcome."

Gemma shot Michael a look as she and Sean walked through the door of Dante's. Maybe coming here wasn't such a great idea. Knowing Michael, he'd be unable to resist swinging by the table repeatedly under the guise of "Making sure everything was all right." As for Anthony, God only knew what could happen. If he was good Anthony, he'd hide in the kitchen and cook. But if he was bad Anthony . . .

The look, mildly withering as intended, appeared to freeze Michael in his tracks. "What?" he asked defensively.

Gemma leaned close to him. "No hovering," she whispered.

Michael put a hand over his heart. "I swear to God, you won't see hide nor hair of me tonight. I'll pretend you don't exist. However, we do need to talk soon."

"About?"

"Nonna."

"Not good?"

Michael frowned. "Not good."

"Call me," Gemma said sadly.

"Will do." He pointed to a large table toward the back where four people already sat chatting. "The other parties have arrived."

"Thanks, Mike," said Sean.

Gemma's hand tightened around Sean's as they walked toward the table. She was so nervous she felt nauseous. She wanted these people to like her. She wanted to like them.

"Do I look okay?" she murmured to Sean.

"Yeah, now that no one's in danger of mistaking you as a Bollywood extra."

"Ass," Gemma whispered affectionately.

Sean squeezed her hand. "Just be yourself and you'll be fine."

"Okay."

"Everyone: This is Gemma."

Four pair of eyes simultaneously swiveled to look at her. "Hi," Gemma said to the party in general as Sean pulled out a chair for her. "It's nice to meet you all."

"You, too," said Mike Leary, previously known as Mustache. His poker face told Gemma he wasn't going to mention meeting her previously, which was fine. "I'm Mike

Leary," he said, then turned to a small, freckled brunette at his side, "and this is my wife, Ronnie."

"Hi," said Ronnie, her eyes doing a sweep of Gemma from head to toe.

The other man at the table, blond, plump, and younger than both Sean and Mike Leary, extended a hand to Gemma. "Hi, I'm Ted Delaney."

"He's a probie," Sean explained.

"He'll be serving us our dinner tonight and mopping up in the kitchen later," Leary joked. All three men laughed. Gemma smiled graciously.

The woman at Delaney's side, also plump and blond, extended a hand to Gemma. "I'm Ted's girlfriend, Danielle. Nice to meet you."

"You, too."

Leary leaned over to Sean. "You know who that is greeting people at the door? *Michael Dante.*" His voice rang with a reverence that made Gemma want to giggle.

Sean turned to Gemma. "Should I tell them, or do you want to do the honors?"

"I'll do it. Michael is my cousin," she told them.

"No shit!" Leary looked impressed.

"He is *hot*," Danielle said dreamily.

"He is," Ronnie Leary agreed. She looked to her husband. "Who is he again?"

"He plays for the New York Blades," Leary explained patiently. "He's one of the toughest SOBs in the NHL."

"He's really a pussycat," Gemma confided. The others all turned to gaze at Michael. Gemma could tell they enjoyed being privy to this piece of private information.

"Hot," Danielle said again.

"Very," Ronnie agreed.

Gemma relaxed a little; Sean's friends seemed nice. The evening would go well. She was sure of it. Then Anthony came bounding out of the kitchen, making a beeline for their table. "*Willkommen. Bienvenue.* Welcome!"

"Mikey already said that."

Anthony scowled. "He did?"

Gemma nodded.

"The little bastard stole my lines!"

"You two know each other?" asked Ronnie Leary.

"He's my cousin, too. In fact, he's Michael's brother. Anthony, say hello to the nice people."

Anthony bowed deeply.

"Good evening, one and all. I'm Anthony Dante, and I'll be your chef this evening. Allow me to tell you of our two specials: We have grilled T-bone steak Florentine style, as well as pan-roasted lamb with juniper berries. Aldo will be by shortly to take your orders." He looked at Gemma. "What should I get you? A tofu dog?"

"Very funny."

Anthony took another bow and disappeared back into the kitchen.

"Tofu dog?" asked Danielle.

"I'm a vegetarian," Gemma explained. "Anthony likes to tease me about it." She saw Ronnie Leary roll her eyes to her husband.

"What made you decide to not eat meat?" Danielle asked.

Beneath the table, Gemma felt Sean's hand squeeze her knee. Gemma squeezed back. "Health reasons."

The waiter swung by with menus, and for a few minutes, the talk was of food. But once drinks were served and dinner ordered, Gemma could feel a certain sense of awkwardness.

"So, Gemma, what do you do?" Ronnie Leary asked.

"I own a shop in Greenwich Village."

"Oohh, la di da," sang Mike Leary.

Gemma shot Sean a quick, quizzical look. Was this guy teasing? Making fun of her? Putting her down? Which? Sean seemed oblivious.

"What kind of shop?" Danielle wanted to know.

Another squeeze from Sean. Unfolding her napkin, Gemma pushed his hand away.

"I sell books, candles, crystals, that kind of thing."

Mike Leary laughed loudly. "People really buy enough of that shit for you to make a living?"

Gemma colored slightly. "Yes."

He nudged Sean in the ribs. "There's one born every minute, huh?" To Gemma's surprise, Sean chuckled his agreement.

"What do you do?" Gemma asked Ronnie Leary.

"I'm a nurse."

"That must be hard work."

"It's hard on the feet, that's for sure."

Gemma brightened, seeing a way to connect. "You know what's good for that? Peppermint oil. Mix a little into some hot water and then soak your feet in it. Works like a charm."

Ronnie looked uncertain. "Um . . . okay."

"I'm not so sure I want a wife with tootsies that smell like candy canes," Mike Leary joshed.

"Like you ever go anywhere near the lower half of my body," Ronnie drawled. Leary turned red and unfurled his napkin with a snap.

Gemma looked away uneasily. She hated couples who aired their dirty laundry in public. Thankfully, the Learys weren't the only ones there. She turned to Danielle. "What do you do?"

"I'm a haircutter." She was eyeing Gemma's tresses with interest.

Mike Leary patted the top of his bald head. "Haven't seen one of those in a while."

Everyone laughed.

"I could fix that, you know," Danielle continued.

Gemma was confused. "Fix what?"

"Your hair. If you let me thin it and shape it—"

"No, thank you," Gemma said politely. Again her eyes

sought Sean's, wondering if he noticed Danielle had just insulted her, though Danielle was clearly unaware of having done so. And again Sean seemed to be just rolling along, listening to conversation.

"So," said Mike Leary, "you all catch 'King of Queens' the other night? It was hilarious."

Spirited discussion ensued and Gemma had no idea what they were talking about. Ted Delaney noticed and asked, "Not a Kevin James fan?"

Gemma smiled apologetically. "I don't know who that is. I don't watch a lot of television."

Conversation died hard, if only for a moment. Gemma felt herself sinking. *They hate me,* she thought miserably. *They think I'm a snobby weirdo who's obsessed with peppermint oil.* The moment was rescued by Sean. "Gemma doesn't watch much TV because she's so busy taking pictures." He beamed at her. "Gemma takes great photos."

"Oh yeah?" Ted Delaney's interest was piqued. "I always wanted to do that, but I could never figure out the f-stops and all that stuff. I'm strictly a point-and-click man now."

"That's why God invented autofocus," said Gemma, happy to be part of the loop.

Then conversation turned to the firehouse and some baseball player named John Franco and she was lost again, reduced to Sean's smiling, silent companion. It didn't help her nerves that Michael appeared every fifteen minutes like clockwork and Anthony could be seen periodically peering out at them from a crack between the swinging doors.

"How we all doing?" Michael asked on what had to be his fifth visit to the table.

Gemma looked up at him imploringly. "We're doing great, Mikey, except for a certain chef who keeps popping his head out the kitchen door to stare at us. Maybe you can fix that?"

"I'll see what I can do," Michael soothed, striding force-fully toward the kitchen and slamming through the swinging doors, where he could be heard bellowing, "Stop staring at Gemma and her boyfriend, you oversized moron!" at the top of his lungs. Naturally, Anthony returned fire.

"Some pussycat," Ronnie Leary noted above the din of pots clattering to the floor.

"Italians are like that," Danielle said knowingly. "Very emotional people."

"Are you Italian?" Gemma asked. Perhaps they'd be able to commiserate about crazy families.

"No, Irish. But I've heard stories. And I watch the *Sopranos*." She looked at Gemma with newfound curiosity. "Do you know anyone in the Mafia?"

"*I'm not sure* your friends liked me," Gemma said un-certainly as she and Sean drove back to Manhattan.

"They liked you fine."

"Then why did Danielle insult my hair? And what was with Mike Leary's 'la di da' when I said I owned my own business?"

"Ah, neither of them meant anything by it," Sean said good-naturedly, reaching across to squeeze her knee. Which reminded Gemma . . .

"Why did you keep squeezing my knee? What did you think I was going to say?"

Sean shrugged. " I don't know. I just thought it was a good idea to keep it light, you know?"

Gemma glanced out the window. "I guess."

"Did you like them?"

"They were nice," Gemma replied carefully.

"Not exactly a ringing endorsement," Sean noted dryly.

"I don't watch TV, Sean. I don't care about baseball. I don't know anyone in the firehouse. I don't know anyone in the Mafia."

"Just relax," said Sean testily. "It'll come."

"What if it doesn't?"

Sean turned his head to look at her. "What does that mean?"

"Nothing. I'm tired. Just forget it."

"How's Peppermint Pattie?"

Sean glanced up from the sports pages of the *Daily News* to see Mike Leary standing over him, stroking his mustache. Dinner was done, the dishwasher was churning away, and most of the guys were gathered around the TV set in the ready room watching a *Sopranos* rerun. It had been a pretty dead shift so far: one false alarm and one trash can fire set by a homeless man up the street.

Sean folded up the paper. "Don't talk about my girl-friend like that."

"Ooh, girlfriend. Owns her own business, too. Seany's got himself a sugar mama, huh?"

"Putting aside the fact that you and your pinky-sized dick are obviously threatened by an independent woman, what did you think of her?"

Leary bit his lip, thoughtful. "Cute. Hair's gotta go, though. They could probably find the Lindbergh baby in there."

"You're such an asshole."

Leary slapped him affectionately on the back. "Ah, I'm just raggin' on ya, you know that. Sometimes—"

He was cut off by the shrill sound of the alarm horn as it blasted through the firehouse.

LADDER TWENTY-NINE, ENGINE THIRTY-ONE, FIRE RE-PORTED AT BROWNSTONE AT 334 EAST SEVENTY-NINTH OFF LEXINGTON AVENUE.

Jumping to his feet, Sean, with Leary right behind him, ran down to the apparatus floor to put on his turnout gear. Sean wondered if the quiet night was about to change.

Adrenaline rushed through him, hot and fast. It didn't matter how long he'd been doing this or how many times he got called out during a shift: It was always a rush, the potential for facing down and conquering unknown danger the most amazing high he knew. Grabbing his tank and helmet, he swung up onto the ladder truck and into the back cabin, lights flashing and siren blaring as they sped out of the engine bay.

Racing to a fire always made him think of Moses and his little trick with the Red Sea: Traffic parted for them as the city flew by the outside window in a blur. In his mind Sean reviewed who'd be doing what. As the Irons Man, Sean would be going interior with Lieutenant Carrey to conduct the primary search. They'd bring Delaney with them, too, for experience's sake. Mike Leary would be handling outside ventilation. Joe Jefferson, the chauffeur, would remain with the truck. "Socrates" Campbell would take care of the roof, cutting a hole for ventilation. Twenty-nine Ladder was a good crew: fast, strong, and competent. Even the battalion chief said so, and he wasn't a man given to high praise.

Sean could smell the smoke as they turned onto East Seventy-ninth. If someone asked him to describe it, he wouldn't be able to, though another firefighter would understand exactly how he could so accurately pinpoint the mixed aromas of burning wood, chemicals, and plaster. By the time they reached the brownstone and he caught sight of the thick black smoke billowing out the second- and third-floor windows of the brownstone, his heart sank. It was gonna be a real job. He hoped to Christ no one was in there.

Jumping off the truck, he waited for instructions from Lieutenant Carrey. As he suspected, he, Carrey, and Delaney were being sent inside to do the primary search. On the sidewalk, a small crowd of neighbors had gathered, their expressions anxious as they watched the guys from Thirty-one Engine unfurl their hoses and charge the lines. A woman in a pink silk dressing gown told Lieutenant Carrey she was pretty sure a child lived in the brownstone. Just a child? Carrey pressed. Two adults and a child, the woman amended. Sean filed the info away as he fixed his mask's face piece to his head and turned on his bottled air. He ran up the front steps and broke down the door with his rabbit tool. Then, bracing himself for his inevitable plunge into the smoky maw, he went inside, following closely behind Carrey.

He was hit immediately with a rolling wall of smoke. The fire, wherever it was, had to be "going good." Dropping to his knees, Sean crawled forward. The heat roiling through the house was intense. With Delaney right behind him, Sean crawled into what he thought was the dining room. Once or twice he stopped, backing up when he didn't feel Delaney's hand on his air tank. The last thing he needed was to lose a probie in smoke as dense as this was.

Sweeping his ax handle in front of him in a slow, back-and-forth motion, Sean gave two quick prayers. One was they wouldn't find anyone in the house. The other that if they did, they'd be able to save them. No one in the dining room, living room, or kitchen. Sean paused as his radio crackled and Carrey's voice came through.

"Battalion Six, this is Ladder Twenty-nine Carrey. Main floor appears to be clear. I'm going up to search the parlor floor with Kennealy and Delaney k."

Sean could barely hear the battalion chief's response on his radio as a deafening crack exploded above him, sending sparks showering down the stairwell. "Ladder Twenty-nine, proceed to parlor floor."

Sean turned around to Delaney. "You doin' okay?" he yelled.

"Great," Delaney yelled back.

Slowly, Sean followed Carrey up the stairs on his hands and knees. The higher they rose, the more intense the heat. Sweat was pouring off his forehead, down the back of his head, rolling down his carefully protected neck. One crack in his protective gear and he had no doubt his neck would be scalded. Black smoke clogged his vision, making progress slow.

The parlor floor clear, Sean waited as Lieutenant Carrey radioed back down to the incident commander that they were going up to the third floor, where most of the bedrooms were. Remembering back to his own days as a probie, Sean was impressed by Ted Delaney's coolness—at his own first major fire, he'd been breathing so hard and heavy he went through his oxygen in fifteen minutes.

They tackled yet another set of steps on all fours. It was like crawling through hell, Sean decided as he slowly edged forward onto the landing. Dark. Like crawling into oblivion. Suddenly Carrey turned to him, speaking through the radio.

"Kennealy, you go search the two front bedrooms and meet me back here at the steps. I'll take Delaney and search the back bedrooms."

"Gotcha."

Crawling down the hallway, Sean felt along the wall until he came to a door frame. Reaching up, he felt for the doorknob and pushed the door open. The room was black as dead of night. Amazing, how there were degrees of darkness, degrees of black. Search clockwise, he reminded himself. Clockwise, clockwise. Where was the goddamn fire? Fourth floor? Where was the kid? His parents? Anyone? Was anyone in the house?

Crawling into the room, Sean felt along the outer wall, hoping to find a window. The wall was hot to the touch; maybe the bastard was within the walls and the ceiling. Moving forward into the deathly darkness, he met resistance. Sean pushed; the obstacle was large and solid, some kind of chifforobe blocking the window. Fuck! He'd have to feel around further, see if there were any other windows in the room he might be able to use for a possible escape.

Fear whispered in his ear, but he pushed the distraction aside as he concentrated on continuing his search of the room, though he knew it could light up at any minute. He crawled forward three steps, his axe handle hitting what appeared to be the leg of a bed. Anxious, he reached up and patted the top. Empty. Did the same thing on the other side of the bed. Still nothing. He checked under the bed: clear. Rising up on his knees, he rolled the mattress back so it was folded in half lengthwise. If any firefighter came in after him, he'd know the room had been searched.

He continued his circuit around the room, encountering a bookshelf and a dresser. At least that's what they felt like. Checked the closet. No one there. Out beyond the door of the bedroom, he heard crackling. Fire had erupted in the hallway. Having completed his circuit of the first bedroom, he crawled forward into the hallway. Flames danced on the ceiling above him, creating an eerie, otherworldly glow in the darkness. Grabbing his can, Sean doused the flames just enough to enable himself to get to the next bedroom. The fire was too big for him to put out. For now, containing it this way would have to do. Besides, he had to look for this kid. *Find the kid.*

The heat was close to unbearable now, visibility a memory. Sean inched forward on his hands and knees, feeling the wall until he came to another door frame. This time the door was open and he crawled right across the threshold. Turning left, Sean immediately made out the shape of a bed. On top of the bed? Nothing. Under the bed? Nothing. He rolled back the mattress and continued on, feeling his way through the darkness. Dresser. Chair. Closet. Ladies dresses. *No kid. No one.* He glanced up: Fire was scorching the bedroom ceiling. As quickly as he could, he crawled back out into the hallway, meeting Lieutenant Carrey and probie Delaney by the stairwell as instructed.

"Both bedrooms are clear," he said. Carrey nodded, getting on his radio.

"Ladder Twenty-nine to Battalion Six. Primary search of the third floor completed. We're going to head on up to four k."

"Battalion Six to Ladder Twenty-nine, this is Murphy. Carrey, I want you and your men to back out now. The fourth floor is about to collapse. Repeat: The fourth floor is about to collapse. Back out NOW."

Shit, Sean thought, looking up from where he crouched on the floor on all fours. Flames were dripping down from the ceiling now like icicles. Any minute, the walls were going to go up. As fast as he could, Sean followed Carrey, and Delaney down. They had just reached the bottom of the steps when a portion of the fourth floor collapsed, sending burning wood and plaster crashing down, a flaming beam missing Sean by mere inches as he, Carrey, and Delaney made it back out through the front door to safety.

Whipping off his breathing apparatus and helmet, he gasped at the fresh air, more out of release than need. A chill shuddered through him as the steaming sweat rising off his body collided with the cool night air. A second later came a roar that sounded as if it had come from the depths of hell itself.

Sean forced his eyes back to the brownstone, watching as the house was consumed with flames. What the hell could have started it? Faulty wiring, a dropped cigarette? He doubted it was arson in a neighborhood like this. Sean checked his watch. They'd been at the scene for less than fifteen minutes.

"Shit."

The fire had been knocked down, and the brownstone had been cleared of smoke. Sean and the rest of the ladder company were doing salvage now, covering intact furniture with tarps to protect it from water and debris, dragging burned items into the street to soak them with water. Hearing Sal Ojeda's exclamation, Sean walked from where he was covering a dresser to see Ojeda standing by a hope chest. The lid was open.

"What?" Sean asked, his heart beginning to punch in his chest.

Ojeda just shook his head and backed away. Sean reached the chest and looked inside.

There, curled up on top of a brightly colored patchwork quilt, was a little boy. A thin layer of soot coated his small body. There was soot around his nose, and the ring of it circling his mouth reminded Sean of a child's sloppily eaten ice cream cone. His blond hair fell across his forehead in wisps, and his hands were clasped together as if in prayer. He looked as though he were sleeping.

"Oh, Christ," Sean whispered. Revulsion at himself bubbled up his throat.

"Sean."

He jerked Ojeda's hand off his shoulder just in time to crouch low as the first wave of vomit spilled from his mouth. *How did I miss the fucking hope chest? Jesus Christ. I let him die. I let that kid die.*

"Wait! I think he's breathin'!"

Sean lifted his head to see Ojeda gingerly lift the boy from the chest and lay him on the ground. Wiping his mouth, he elbowed Ojeda out of the way. Tilting the boy's head back, he put his hand in the boy's mouth to make sure all was clear. Then he pinched his nostrils and began administering CPR.

"Breathe!" Sean yelled as he switched from breathing into the boy's mouth to compressing his chest with the heel of one hand. He gave five small pumps. "Don't you fuckin' die on me, kid! C'mon!"

His mouth returned to the boy's. Breathe. Pump five. Breathe. Pump five. Breathe.

"Sean!"

Sean looked up to see an EMT frantically racing toward him.

"Let me take over!"

"Sean, come on." It was Captain McCloskey. "Devlin can take it from here. There's an ambulance on the way. Go back and wait in the truck. We're almost done here."

Heart hammering in his chest, Sean did as he was told.

Back at the firehouse, Sean's shift was ending and he was getting ready to leave. Even though Carrey had done a quick diffusing at the scene, there was still going to be a debriefing at the firehouse the next day. Everyone at the fire scene would be asked to talk about what they did and how they felt about what happened. Self-loathing seized Sean just thinking about it. *I fucked up. How the hell do you think I feel about it?* he imagined himself sneering at the facilitating firefighter, who would be brought in from another house.

"Kennealy, come here a minute," said Carrey.

Obeying his lieutenant's wishes, Sean approached Carrey where he sat on the shiny chrome bumper of the engine truck. "What's up?"

"Look, I know what you're thinking right now. You're thinking you're a fuckup. You're beating yourself up for missing that hope chest."

"Pretty much."

"Well, I'm here to tell you it could have happened to any one of us. It has nothing to do with your skill as a fire-fighter."

Yeah, right.

"Shit like this happens, Sean. Just be grateful the kid's still alive."

"He at Lenox Hill?"

Carrey nodded.

"I might head over there tomorrow. See if he's okay."

"Good idea. It might make you feel better. Just try not to dwell on this or it'll make you nuts. You know you can talk to me if you need to, right?"

"Yeah."

"You know there's a mental health unit, too, and—"

"I'm fine," Sean cut in. "No offense, but I'm fine."

"Okay." Sean could tell Carrey didn't believe him, but he wasn't going to pursue the point any further. He clapped Sean on the shoulder. "Go home and try to get some rest. It's been one long fuckin' night."

"You got that right," Sean muttered.

"His friend actually said 'La di da' when you told him you owned a store?"

"Yup."

"Sounds like a jerk."

Gemma didn't disagree as she followed Frankie to the next street vendor, this one selling colorful handwoven sweaters from Guatemala. They were at the Park Avenue South Autumn Fair, waiting for Sean to show. Though a dinner date had been set the following week for Sean to meet her friends, she wanted him to meet Frankie alone first. It was important to Gemma that her best friend and her boyfriend get along.

"Did you at least have fun?"

"I don't know if 'fun' is the word I'd use." Gemma lifted the arm of a sweater, rubbing the material between her fingers. "It was . . . illuminating." The sleeve felt scratchy. She let it drop.

"Illuminating. Haven't heard that one in a while." Frankie strolled on to the next booth, where a squat, un-

smiling couple in matching blue polyester sat selling paintings done on black velvet. She pointed to a large rectangu-
lar portrait of John Wayne beaming down from heaven on
a circling wagon train. "What do you think?"

Gemma watched as Frankie casually forked over forty
dollars, tucking the painting under her arm. "They were
really nice people—apart from insulting me about my hair
and the store, of course." Thinking about it, Gemma's
heart sank a little. "This is going to cause problems. It *is*
causing problems. They were talking about TV shows and
someone named John Franco and I was totally lost. I mean,
I couldn't contribute *anything*. I think they thought I was
kind of weird."

"You are. But in a good way."

Gemma frowned. "That's not helpful. I don't think
'weirdness' is high on Sean's list of qualities he's looking
for in a girlfriend."

They were about to walk on when Gemma heard her
name called. She turned. Uther was strolling toward her, a
big smile on his pale face. *Perfect,* she thought.

"Hey, you." Gemma motioned him over. "Uther, I want
you to meet my best friend, Frankie Hoffmann. Frankie,
this is Uther Abramowitz. I'm teaching him tarot."

Uther's smile was pleasant as he shook Frankie's hand.
"Nice surprise to see you here," he said to Gemma.

"We're waiting for her boyfriend," Frankie explained.

Uther's face fell slightly. "Oh."

"Uther's that student of mine I was telling you about,"
Gemma said quickly, fumbling to salvage the moment.
"You know, with the photographic memory?"

Frankie nodded. "Yes, I remember. Very cool. Comput-
ers, right?"

Uther narrowed his eyes, intrigued. "And you're—?"

"A DJ," Frankie replied in her Lady Midnight voice.
"WROX, the city's best rock."

Gemma suppressed a laugh. She'd seen Frankie per-
form this trick a hundred times, and it always had the same
effect: Men went weak in the knees. Uther was no exception. Blood flooded his face and, Gemma imagined, other
parts of his body she didn't want to think of.

"Your voice is like the song of the nightingale," Uther
said rapturously. "I listen to you all the time!"

"Of course you do." Frankie gestured to the black plastic bag in Uther's hand. "Whatcha got there?"

Uther opened the bag, pulling out a chain mail tunic.
Gemma and Frankie just stared.

"I'm a medieval reenactor in my spare time. We're stag-
ing the Battle of Hastings in Central Park next Sunday."
His eyes brushed Frankie's. "You should come."

"Maybe I will," Frankie purred.

Gemma's heart gave a small leap of glee. A medieval
reenactor! This was eccentric enough to be right up
Frankie's alley. She had no doubt she could bring the two
together. She tugged Frankie's sleeve.

"We should get going." She smiled at Uther. "Tuesday?"

"As ever, madam." He bowed deeply before Frankie.
"Charmed to have made your acquaintance, m'lady." With
that he shimmied off.

"What did you think?"

Frankie pursed her lips thoughtfully. "Kinda cute in a
Renaissance Fair kind of way, you know?"

"So I can give him your number if he asks?"

Frankie shrugged. "Why not? There are worse things in
life than dating a guy who dresses up and pretends he's
William the Conqueror." She glanced down at her watch.
"Honey, your man is L-A-T-E. He was supposed to meet
us twenty minutes ago."

"I know." Gemma fought rising embarrassment as they
strolled along to the next vendor. It wasn't like Sean to be
late. He must have encountered heavy traffic. Or maybe he

forgot to set his alarm. She hadn't talked to him since he'd left for his shift the night before.

As they strolled past a booth selling chunky turquoise belts and rings, Gemma's eye was drawn to a newspaper tossed on an empty chair: FIRE RIPS THROUGH UPPER EAST SIDE BROWNSTONE, the headline read. ONE INJURED.

"Oh, God." Gemma approached the vendor, who was showing a potential customer a necklace. "Can I see your paper? Please?"

The vendor nodded and Gemma rushed into the booth to retrieve the paper. Hands trembling, she opened to the story. A black-and-white photo of the brownstone's charred remains jumped out at her, sending her stomach plummeting to her feet. *Sean.* Mouth dry, she quickly skimmed the text. As soon as she saw the words *Ladder Twenty-nine*, she stopped.

"I have to go."

"What?" Frankie looked confused as Gemma handed her the paper and began anxiously pacing in place like some caged animal. Frankie read fast. "You're sure it was Sean's firehouse who handled this fire?"

Gemma nodded, blinking back tears. "Yes. What if something's happened to him?"

"Calm down. You're making yourself crazy over nothing. The article said it was a kid who was hospitalized, not a firefighter."

"So? That doesn't mean anything!"

"Maybe he's just delayed. " Frankie looked genuinely concerned. "Gemma, you have to calm down. You're acting nuts."

"I feel nuts." Gemma stopped pacing and folded her arms tightly across her chest. "Every time he walks out the door, I get this scared, sick feeling: what if, what if. I can't take it."

"Clearly." Frankie pulled her aside so they were out of

the way of foot traffic. "What do you want to do?" she asked, wrapping an arm around Gemma's shoulder.

"Call him. I don't know."

"How about this: Why don't we wait another half hour or so, and if he doesn't show up, then you call him, or go home, or whatever. Does that sound good?"

"Okay."

"I can't believe he stood me up on our first date," Frankie joked with a smile, trying to lighten things up.

Gemma tried returning the gesture, but her smile wouldn't come.

Wake up. Wake up so I can see you with your eyes open and believe you're really alive. Wake up.

Sitting alongside the hospital bed of the little boy who'd hidden in the chest, Sean tried to will him awake. The boy had a name, Jason Duffy, and according to the nurses, he'd suffered severe smoke inhalation but otherwise appeared to be "fine," meaning no brain damage from lack of oxygen as far as the doctors could tell. Unlike the staff at O'Toole's, the nurses had Lenox Hill had a soft spot for firefighters; all Sean had to do was tell them who he was and they let him in, no questions asked, despite the fact it was nowhere near visiting hours. Of course, he felt like a fraud telling them he'd saved the boy's life. It was his fault the kid was here, but he'd deal with his self-loathing later. For now, it was crucial he see the child alive.

He moved his chair an inch closer to the bed, the better to watch the rise and fall of the boy's chest. The room was eerily quiet, TV on but sound off, the silent image of Big Bird flickering across the small screen mounted up near the ceiling. In the next bed lay another little boy who'd undergone an appendectomy. Every time he groaned, "It hurts . . . it hurts," Sean's guts twisted. There was nothing worse than kids in pain.

He'd gone right home after his shift, but was unable to sleep. His mind kept insisting he revisit the brownstone fire. How could he have missed the chest during the primary search? It was so basic it was embarrassing. He was haunted by the image of the boy lying curled up inside. Had Ojeda waited two more minutes to crack it open, the kid would be dead. Eventually he had put his clothes back on and headed over to Lenox Hill. He had to see with his own eyes that his negligence hadn't killed the child.

And now here he was, keeping silent vigil. From what he'd been able to gather from his lieutenant, the boy's parents had been out at a party when the fire started. The babysitter called 911 and then fled the house, leaving the little boy inside. The source of the fire had yet to be determined.

Things like this happen, Lieu had said, referring to Sean's fuck-up. *Just be grateful the kid's alive.* Sean was grateful. Of course he was. But he was also deeply ashamed and shaken. He'd never messed up this badly before. Ever. Yeah, shit happens, but this was major, this was inexcusable. Telling him not to beat himself up was a joke. How could he not? Staring into Jason Duffy's sleeping face, all he could think was: *I almost killed him.* Not "Thank God we found him in time," but "I almost killed him." How was he supposed to live with that?

The boy stirred. *Please wake up. Please.* But he was only shifting position in his sleep. Sean sat beside him another half hour. Then he made himself go. Were it up to him, he'd sit here all day and night. He'd stay until the boy was discharged. Crazy, but he couldn't help it. He felt responsible for the boy's condition. He was responsible.

It wasn't until he was back outside in the sunshine that he remembered he was supposed to meet Gemma and her friend at the street fair. He checked his watch. He was over an hour late. They'd probably left by now, so he headed for home. Now that he'd seen the boy with his own eyes,

maybe he'd be able to catch some sleep. Maybe. Gemma
would just have to understand.

At the sound of locks being clicked back, Gemma flew
off the couch. She and Sean had given each other keys to
one another's apartment, and Gemma took advantage of
the privilege, using her key to let herself into Sean's place
to wait for him. An anguished cry slipped from her lips at
the sight of him walking through the doorway, weary but
clearly all right. Running to him, she crushed him to her,
hugging him, kissing him, frantic, grateful.

"Hey." Troubled, Sean gently disentangled himself
from her grasp and looked down into her eyes. "What's
going on?"

Gemma began to cry. "That brownstone fire—you were
there, weren't you? And when you didn't show at the
fair . . ."

"Sshh, come here." He took her in his arms. "I'm sorry
I missed the fair. I had to go visit someone in the hospital."

Gemma swiped at her eyes. "Who?"

Sean swallowed. "A little boy."

"The little boy from the fire?"

"Yeah." He drifted from her embrace and sank down on
the couch. "I'm exhausted."

"Is the little boy okay?"

"He's fine."

Gemma approached the couch. "Are you okay?"

"I'm fine."

Gemma wrung her hands helplessly. "I was so worried."

"You always are." There was annoyance in his bloodshot eyes. "You know, if you're gonna freak out every tim
I get called to a fire—"

"I can't help it," Gemma interrupted quietly. "I ca
about you."

Sean rubbed his eyes vigorously with the heels of his palms. "I know you do, Gem, but it makes me feel pressured. I've got enough shit to worry about without worrying that you're losing it every time I go to work."

"I'm sorry."

She knew Sean was right, but his testiness still hurt.

"I'm sorry, too." He held his hand out to her, and Gemma joined him on the couch. "Does your friend hate me?"

"Of course not. You'll just meet her next Saturday night, that's all."

Sean's face was a blank.

"Dinner? My apartment? With my friends?" Gemma prompted.

"Right, right." He let his head drop back, staring up at the ceiling. "That's next week?"

"Yes." Gemma tensed slightly. "It's not a problem, is it? I thought we agreed—"

"It's fine. I'm just tired and my sense of time is off."

"Are you sure you're okay?' Gemma asked, smoothing his brow. She knew she was pushing. She could feel it. But she couldn't help it. Maybe it was in Sean's mother's nature to let things go. But she was a Dante. She couldn't. If her man was in pain, she wanted to know. She wanted to help.

Sean slowly lifted his head from the back of the couch to look at her. "I could have sworn I already answered that question."

Gemma backed off. "You did. I'm sorry."

Sean rose with a heavy sigh. "I'm sorry, babe, but I have to crash. Now."

"I understand." Gemma slid off the couch. "Want me to tuck you in?"

Sean shook his head. "Nah, you go on downstairs. I'll call you when I wake up, okay?"

Gemma stood on tiptoes to kiss his cheek. "I'm very proud of you, Sean."

"What do you mean?"

"Proud of what you do. And that you're the kind of man who goes to visit kids in the hospital. He wouldn't be alive if it wasn't for you."

Pain cracked behind Sean's eyes. "Right. I'm a real hero."

Without another word, he kissed her forehead and went into the bedroom, closing the door behind him.

CHAPTER

12

Urging himself down the one flight of stairs to Gemma's apartment, Sean was in no mood to socialize; hadn't been all week. Part of it was insomnia: Every time he closed his eyes, he was back at the brownstone, and if there was one thing that made him ornery, it was lack of sleep. But mostly, he just had an overwhelming urge to withdraw—from people, from places, from all the vicissitudes of daily life.

Simply put, he wanted to be left the hell alone.

Still, he knew it was important to Gemma that he meet her friends. He was determined to push himself through the evening, the same way he was pushing himself through life these days. He knocked on the door. The sight of Gemma, radiant in her purple sari, made him smile. He was pleased to note he could still feel. He leaned in for a quick kiss.

"Am I late?"

"Perfect timing," she murmured, leading him by the hand into the living room. The quiet buzz of conversation slowly faded as a tall, gangly blonde with a patch over her left eye; a slight, platinum-haired man clad all in black; and a handsome young man who looked like a Hispanic Errol Flynn all watched him approach.

"Everyone, I want you to meet Sean." There was excitement in Gemma's voice as she led him to the blond woman, who looked like Heidi turned pirate. "This is Frankie."

Sean extended a hand, flashing his most charming smile. "Nice to meet you."

"You, too." Frankie tapped the eye patch. "Scratched cornea. David Crosby threw a paper airplane at me in the studio."

"Does this mean your cataracts have cleared up?" Gemma inquired sweetly.

Frankie flashed Gemma a scowl.

Sean thought it was pretty cool that Frankie got to rub elbows with rock stars. He made a mental note to ask her about it later.

Still holding his hand, Gemma led him next to the man in black. Sean toyed with making a Johnny Cash joke, then thought better of it. This guy didn't seem like someone you could rib.

"Sean, this is Theo."

"Tay—oh," he corrected crossly.

Gemma put an apologetic hand over her heart. "Sorry, I mean Tay-oh. I can't keep track of your ever-changing names. Theo's a performance artist."

"Nice to meet you," Sean said again, reaching out to shake Tay-oh's hand. He couldn't wait to get this guy's story.

"Last but not least, this is Miguel. He's the fashion editor at *Verve*."

"*Enchanté,*" Miguel purred, dark eyes flashing. "You're the fireman, right?" Sean nodded. "Mmm, I love a man in uniform."

"Behave," Gemma chastised affectionately. She squeezed Sean's hand. "What can I get you to drink?"

"A Guinness would be great." He settled down on the couch beside Frankie.

"Oh." Gemma seemed at a loss. "Sweetie, I forgot to get beer."

"No problem." *You know that's the only alcohol I drink, but hey, that's okay.* "I'll drink what everyone else is drinking."

"You won't regret it," Miguel assured him. "Gemma's mixed up the most divine margaritas."

"A margarita sounds great."

Gemma flashed him a happy smile as she scurried into the kitchen, leaving Sean to wonder whose responsibility it was to pick up the conversational ball. He decided to take the bull by the horns.

"I know you and Gemma have been friends since you were kids," he said to Frankie. He turned to the two men. "But how do you guys know her?"

Theo sighed. "We met many, many moons ago when we were in the same coven."

"Really." *Just what I wanted to hear. File that under "Info never to be repeated."*

"Yes, but it wasn't her cup of tea, though we all adored her. She's clearly a solitary."

Sean nodded. "And are you still—er—"

"Pagan? Dear God, no. That was just a step in my evolution as an artist." Miguel snickered and Theo turned to him furiously. "Up your hole with a Mello roll."

Miguel rolled his eyes dramatically. "Theo's very touchy about his art."

"I'd like to hear about it," said Sean, trying to sound friendly and encouraging. He was having a hard time getting a handle on these guys. *Are they a couple? Did they used to be a couple?* Gemma hadn't said. His fingers itched for a drink.

Theo's expression was earnest. "My performances explore the oppression of man in an increasingly gynocentric society."

Sean's brows knit together so hard it hurt. "Excuse me?"

Miguel chuckled meanly. "He wishes he had a hoo-hoo."

Before Sean could respond—not that he was sure there was a response to that—Gemma swept back into the room and handed him his margarita, saving him. "Here you go."

"Thanks." He held his cocktail glass aloft. "To friends."

"To friends," everyone echoed.

"What did I miss?" Gemma asked brightly as she cozied up to Sean.

"I was just getting the lowdown on how everyone knows you," Sean explained. "It's Miguel's turn."

Miguel peered at Gemma quizzically. "Sister woman, how did we meet? Do you remember?"

"Yes. We both wanted that royal blue boa at Screaming Mimi's. We nearly came to blows over it."

"Thaaat's right. I won, if I recall correctly."

"Only because I let you."

"So generous." He blew Gemma an air kiss. *Pretentious twit,* thought Sean.

"Screw boas, I want to hear about firefighting!" Frankie exclaimed.

Sean instinctively stiffened. "What about it?"

"It must be interesting."

"It is." *But please don't ask me if I've ever saved anyone's life.*

Miguel flicked a piece of lint off his trousers. "You must get dirty a lot."

"Yup."

Miguel pursed his lips. "I don't think I'd like that very much."

Theo snorted. "Oh, puh-lease. You go into cardiac arrest if you're within ten feet of dirt."

Miguel shuddered. "That's why I hate the country."

Sean concentrated on his drink. What the hell did you say to something like that? You could challenge the guy, sure, but where would it lead? To some bitchy witticism that would leave him feeling like a schmuck. Not worth it.

Putting down her drink, Gemma reached forward to grab the tray of crudités and hummus from the coffee table and started passing them around. "Did I tell you guys Sean was on Wall Street before he was a firefighter?"

Theo looked bored. "About a hundred times."

Sean shot Gemma a questioning look. *What, being a firefighter isn't good enough?* He reached for a carrot and, swiping it in the hummus, popped it in his mouth. "Great hummus, babe."

"I love when men call women 'babe,'" Miguel sighed. "It's so Neil Diamond."

"Neil Diamond wears so much cologne he could choke a train car," cracked Frankie.

Finally, a line of conversation Sean could get interested in. "You've met Neil Diamond?"

"She's met 'em all, honey." Miguel smirked.

"Yeah?" Sean turned to Frankie. "Mick Jagger?"

"Swears by Elizabeth Arden."

"Steven Tyler?"

"Borrowed my favorite scarf and never gave it back."

"Bruce?"

Frankie groaned. "What is it with firefighters and Bruce? They all love Bruce."

"He sings their pain," mocked Theo.

Sean felt a rush of anger but he beat it back. "Tell me about Bruce," he urged Frankie, consciously ignoring Theo.

"Bruce is really nice, really down to earth."

"He needs a makeover," Miguel opined. "I mean, *hello,* men over fifty in tight black jeans? Pa—the—tique. And that cross he sometimes wears around his neck? So 2003."

Time to tune out, Sean told himself, practically chugging his margarita. He stayed that way for most of the evening, dinner included, which was vegetarian, of course. It was the best way for him to cope with conversation about designers he'd never heard of and defacing Tampon ads and calling it art. He did tune back in once in a while to hear what Frankie had to say about radio and the music business. She was the only one of Gemma's three friends who seemed genuinely interested in him. A little weird—what's with the eye patch?—but friendly and clearly devoted to Gemma. The other two? Stuck-up, self-absorbed assholes. As he watched Gemma laugh and chat with them over the course of the evening, his guts churned a little. *Who is she? What is she doing being friendly with them? And what is she doing with me?*

"**You were quiet** tonight," Gemma observed as she put the last of the leftovers into the fridge.

Sean shrugged. "I guess." He handed her the glass he was drying, glad the cleanup hadn't taken too long. He was exhausted. What little energy he'd started the evening with was completely drained by having to feign cordiality toward Tay-oh the A-ho and Miguel.

Gemma touched his arm. "You okay?"

"Why do you keep asking me that?"

Gemma looked stung. "I don't."

"You do. Constantly. Is there something I'm saying or doing that would lead you to think I'm not okay?"

Gemma paused. "You've been a little off this week."

" 'Off'? What does that mean?"

"Moody. Quiet. Uncommunicative."

"Maybe I'm just a moody, quiet, uncommunicative guy."

"Maybe." Gemma sounded uncertain as she moved to put some more glasses away. "You and Frankie seemed to get along well."

"Yeah, I liked Frankie," said Sean, taking over so Gemma wouldn't have drag out her step stool.

"She seemed to like you. I'm sure she'll give me the full report on the phone tomorrow."

Sean chuckled.

"I think Miguel and Theo liked you, too," Gemma said tentatively.

"Hard to tell, since all they did was talk about themselves." Sean could feel the last ounce of patience drain from his body.

Gemma sighed. "I know. They were a bit over the top tonight."

"You mean they're not always like that?" Sean asked.

"God, no. Be thankful: At least they spared you their dueling Liza Minnelli impersonations."

Sean looked stricken.

"That was a joke, honey. Relax. I think they were deliberately trying to scare you off."

"Why's that?"

"They don't like to share me. I'm going to call both of them tomorrow and tell them they were very naughty boys."

"Good. Because I have to tell you, my initial impression was that Miguel's a nasty queen and Tay-oh is a pretentious ass. I was having a tough time understanding why you're friends with them."

Gemma looked taken aback. "They weren't *that* bad."

Sean snorted. "That's debatable."

"At least they're interesting," Gemma blurted defensively.

"And my friends aren't?" Sean felt his blood pressure surge when Gemma looked away guiltily. "I don't believe you! At least my friends are down to earth!"

"So? That doesn't mean they're interesting!" Gemma slammed the cabinet door shut.

"Oh, excuse me. I guess being a firefighter and saving

people's lives is boring. I guess being a nurse is boring, too.
And a haircutter. At least my friends are doing something
meaningful with their lives! At least they contribute!"

"Why are you being so critical?"

"I'm not being critical, I'm being honest. They're jerks,
Gemma."

"Well, your friends watch stupid, mind-numbing shows
on TV and baseball and think it's funny to insult someone
who runs their own business!" Gemma countered hotly.

Sean chuckled softly. "That says it all."

"I think your friends are nice," was Gemma's lame
comeback. "I just—"

Sean held up a hand. "Never mind. Let's just drop it, all
right? I'm too damn tired." He took the plate Gemma
passed him and stacked it in the cabinet. "One thing,
though: Why did you make such a big deal of my being a
stockbroker before I was a firefighter?"

"I didn't make a big deal of it. I just thought it was interesting, that's all."

"Yeah?"

Gemma looked at him warily. "What are you getting at?"

"You sure you didn't tell them I used to be on Wall
Street because you didn't want them to think I was a plain,
dumb firefighter who listens to Bruce and drinks beer?"

Gemma looked on the verge of tears. "Does that really
sound like something I would do?"

The plaintiveness in her voice cut him. He knew he was
being a prick. "I don't know."

"Well, I wouldn't. And if you think I would, then you
don't know me at all." She put the last of the dishes away.

Sean wished he could open a window and let the tension
just waft away. Or better yet, turn back the clock a few minutes and lie politely, telling her he thought the evening went
well. But he couldn't. His eye caught Gemma's; she was
feeling it, too, the estrangement, the sense of dislocation.

"So, now what?" he offered glumly.

Gemma covered a yawn with her hand. "I'm exhausted. Let's go to bed."

"Actually," said Sean, "I'm going to sleep at my own place tonight, if you don't mind."

"Oh."

How, Sean wondered, could such a little word ring with both surprise and pain?

"Don't worry, nothing's wrong," he assured her, drawing her into an embrace. "I just haven't been sleeping well and I do better in my own bed. You know that."

"No problem." Gemma gently cupped his face with her hand. "Why aren't you sleeping?"

Sean broke away. "Stuff. You know."

"Sean—"

"Gemma. " His voice rang with warning. "Let it go, baby, okay?" He twined his fingers through hers, pressing his lips tenderly to her forehead. "I'll give you a call tomorrow after my shift. Maybe we'll drive out to the beach."

"That would be nice," Gemma replied in a thoroughly noncommittal voice—the same voice she'd used after their disastrous date at O'Toole's.

Another kiss and he was out the door, back upstairs to his own place. *Thank God that's over with,* he thought to himself, reflecting back on dinner. Stripping off, he slid between the sheets and closed his eyes, expecting sleep to hit him like a prizefighter throwing the final victorious punch. Instead, he was back at the brownstone, and when he wasn't there, his mind was chasing itself thinking about Gemma. Sleep never came.

Sean didn't call the next day. Or the next. Uneasy, Gemma left him a message—just one—though she knew he might accuse her of worrying over trifles. When another day passed and he didn't call back, she called an emergency meeting at the diner with Frankie.

"I have to tell you, I don't think it looks good." Frankie sounded like a doctor delivering bad news to a patient. "First he tells you not to tell his folks you're a witch, then he doesn't like your friends—except me, of course"—she added happily—"and to top it all off, he passes up an opportunity for sex?" Frankie shook her head. "Not good."

"He hasn't been himself since that brownstone fire. Not that I can get him to talk about it."

"This goes beyond the brownstone fire."

"I know, I know." Gemma picked listlessly at the English muffin on her plate. "What do you think I should do?"

"That's obvious: Knock on his door and find out what the hell is going on."

"You don't think that's too pushy?"

"Pushy? Gemma, this is your boyfriend we're talking about here. If my boyfriend went AWOL for three days and didn't return my calls, you can bet your butt I'd be pounding on his door. You deserve an explanation."

"I know. I'm just not sure I want to hear what it is."

"Hang on."

Sean's voice through the closed door sounded put-upon. Gemma tensed, not knowing what to expect. The knuckles of her right hand were throbbing. Two more minutes and she would have called the fire department to break in. Talk about irony.

The door swung open, and there stood Sean. He looked like he hadn't slept in days.

"Come on in," he said in a flat voice. Apprehensive, Gemma followed him inside, surprised to see Pete and Roger's cages covered in the middle of the day. Usually, when Sean was up, the birds were, too.

"I've been worried," she told him.

"I know." He sounded weary. "I've been meaning to call you back, I just . . ." He licked his lips, looking lost. "Have a seat."

Gemma sat down, unable to take her eyes off him. "What's going on, Sean?"

"I'm not feeling too well."

"Flu?"

He laughed bitterly. "I wish."

He flopped down in a chair opposite her. She couldn't believe how awful he looked. His lively blue eyes were shockingly lackluster, ringed with dark circles. Three days' worth of stubble grizzled his face and neck. He looked more than sick; he looked tormented.

"Talk to me, Sean."

"About what?"

Gemma worked to keep her voice gentle. "Why haven't you returned my calls?"

"I told you: I haven't been feeling too hot."

"Physically or mentally?"

His eyes slowly rose to hers. "Both, actually."

Gemma knit her hands together. "Does this have anything to do with that brownstone fire?"

"Does what have to do with it?"

"You're not feeling well," Gemma said carefully.

Sean leaned back in his chair, sighing. "No."

She studied his face: the haunted eyes, the pale skin. "You're lying."

"You're right. I am."

"Oh, Sean." She wanted to go to him but his expression—remote, inaccessible—stopped her.

"I don't want to talk about it, Gemma."

"Sean." Her voice bordered on a plea. "There's no need to suffer alone. I'm here for you, I'll listen."

"I just said I don't want to talk about it."

"You might feel better if you do."

"How would you know?" Sean sneered. He gave a short, staccato laugh. "I mean, what the fuck do you know about searching a house, thinking you did a good job, then finding out later you almost left a kid to burn?"

Gemma flinched. *So that's what happened.* "I don't." Her eyes began filling with tears. "But I'm here for you. Please, let me help you."

"There's nothing you can do," Sean said woodenly.

"I can hold you. I can listen."

"I'm fine," Sean insisted through clenched teeth.

"Cutting yourself off from people is not 'fine.'" She twisted her hands helplessly. "Have you been calling in sick to work?"

"What?" He frowned. "No. I pulled a forty-eight-hour shift, so now I'm off for seven days."

"When do you go back?"

"Sunday."

"And what are you going to do until then? Hide in here and play it over and over again in your mind?"

"Maybe," Sean mused bitterly, looking away. When he looked back at her, Gemma got the sense that, right now, the simplest human interaction took tremendous emotional effort for him. He could barely meet her eyes. "Look, I'm not sure this is working for me right now."

Alarm shot through Gemma. "'This'?"

"Us. I don't like your friends and you don't like mine. You can't deal with the facts of my job and frankly, if we're being honest here, your being a witch is just a little too weird for me. Face it, Gemma: The only place we work is in bed."

Tears threatened but Gemma held them back. "That's not true," she said quietly.

"Yeah, babe, it is."

"So, what are you saying?" Gemma struggled to keep her voice from getting shrill or desperate. "You want to split up?"

Sean looked pained. "For now, yeah, maybe."

"For now?" Gemma couldn't believe what she was hearing. "What, I'm supposed to be at your beck and call when and if you change your mind?"

"No."

"Then what?"

"I don't know," Sean groaned, clutching his head. "I can't even think straight right now."

"Well, think about this: Either we're together, or we're apart. You choose."

Sean hung his head. "I think you better go."

Shaking, Gemma slowly stood. "You're sure about this?"

"I just told you I can't even think straight right now!" Sean snapped. His face was a map of misery. "Look, just do whatever the hell you want, okay?"

Gemma moved toward the door, taking back the key to her apartment that lay on a small side table. She was determined to at least hold her tears until she was back at her place. She thought of slamming the door, or just leaving without a word, but that wasn't who she was, and she didn't wish to leave things that way. Instead, she made herself turn back to face him.

"Take care of yourself, Sean. Please." She returned his key.

Sean jerked his head in an approximation of a nod, refusing to look at her.

She slipped through the door without a word more.

CHAPTER

13

He hadn't planned to tell her he wanted to take a break.

He'd been pissed off yesterday when he'd first heard her knocking at the door, but he knew he owed her an explanation, however lame. He just wasn't prepared for how raw he felt, how resentful, at being asked to talk about the brownstone fire; at being asked to talk, period. He knew she meant well, and she was simply reacting to the sight of him in pain. But it angered him rather than making him feel appreciative. It felt like intrusion. Then the words slipped out, a by-product of his bottled-up anger and confusion. But now that she'd granted his wish—permanently, he guessed—he wondered if it had been the right thing to do.

Forcing himself up and out of bed, he went to the kitchen to make some coffee and feed his birds. He had to face the outside world today: There was a retirement party for one of the guys at 49 Engine, and if he didn't show, he'd never hear the end of it. He'd go, have a beer, offer his congrats, then crawl back into his cave.

Anything was endurable for half an hour.

"No offense, but you look like shit."

"Nice to see you, too," Sean replied to Mike Leary as he walked into the Huntington Elks Club. The place was packed with firefighters and their families. The man of the hour, Dennis McNab, was holding court at a long table in the front of the room with some of the guys from his company. Raucous laughter was the soundtrack of the day, making Sean feel even worse for being such a sad sack.

"Where's Rapunzel?"

Sean frowned. "You're friggin' relentless, you know that?" In no mood to tell Leary about the breakup, he thought fast. It was Saturday afternoon. "She's at her store. Couldn't get anyone to fill in for her."

"What's the name of the store again? I'd love to check it out."

Sean pretended he didn't hear as he drifted away. That was the last thing he needed: Mike Leary checking out the Golden Bough, scoping out all the weird stuff Gemma sold. He could just imagine the tales Leary would tell back at the firehouse.

He made his way to one of the coolers and pulled out a Guinness. Scanning the room, he spotted JJ Roper sitting alone off in a corner. JJ, one of the handful of women in the FDNY, entered the fire academy the same time as Sean. But unlike Sean, she had yet to be truly accepted by the guys in her house. Sean had heard more than one firefighter express relief there wasn't a woman at their house. It would change the whole dynamic, some guys claimed. We'd have to watch our mouths and take the porn out of the bathroom, others pointed out. A few even doubted women could pull their weight on the job, despite evidence to the contrary. Sean figured guys were threatened by JJ. She was strong as a horse and totally competent, but she was also drop-dead gorgeous, with legs up to her neck and cascading blond hair she usually wore back in a braid. If she heard half the sexual innuendo she generated, the department would find itself with a major harassment suit. He felt bad seeing her sitting there alone, her outsider status obviously still intact. He decided to join her.

"Hey."

"Hey." JJ's smile was grateful as Sean sat down beside her. "I didn't expect to see you here."

"What, are you kidding me? Miss Nabby's retirement? Not for the world."

JJ looked to the front of the room at the man in question. "What's he going to do now, I wonder?"

"His brother's a contractor. Nabby's been working for him on the side for years. I think he's gonna work with him full-time now."

"And how does Mrs. Nabby feel about that, I wonder?"

"Mr. and Mrs. Nabby split up about seven month ago, I believe."

"Really? A divorced firefighter? That's hard to believe." Her laugh was hard as she drained her drink.

Her bitterness caught Sean's attention. "Trouble at home?" His eyes did a quick scan of the room. "Where's Chris?"

Chris was JJ's husband. In addition to being a prick of world renown, he was also a cop. Lots of cops secretly longed to be firefighters, and the animosity between the two professions was strong. The annual hockey game between the two departments' teams was always a bloodbath. It wasn't uncommon for JJ to bring Chris to firefighter functions and the evening to end in fisticuffs.

"He's on duty, making the world safe for democracy."

"Am I detecting a little sarcasm here?"

"A little."

"What's up?"

JJ held up a hand as if to say, "Wait a minute," and jogged off to refill her drink. "You sure you want to hear this?" she asked Sean when she returned.

"Sure, as long as it's not X-rated."

"It's not." She sipped from her plastic cup. "I want a baby and Chris doesn't. And he wants me to quit the department. Says it's too dangerous."

Sean shook his head, guffawing loudly. "Jesus. I wonder if he's related to my gi—ex-girlfriend." *Ex-girlfriend.* It felt odd even saying it to himself.

JJ looked at him with newfound interest. "I didn't know you had a girlfriend."

"I did, until yesterday."

"What happened?"

Sean shrugged, not exactly eager to talk about it. "She couldn't handle my being a firefighter, among other things." He glanced away. "We just didn't work as a couple, you know? It's hard to explain."

"That's too bad."

"Yeah, it is."

Her expression changed to one of concern. "You look really awful, you know."

"Thanks. You're the second person in less than ten minutes to tell me that."

"Aren't you sleeping?"

"Not much."

There was a split second of hesitation before she asked, "Does this have to do with the brownstone fire?"

Sean slumped against the wall miserably. "Maybe. What have you heard?"

JJ looked uncomfortable. "You know. The kid. The chest."

Sean glanced at her sharply. "So word's gotten around I'm a fuckup."

JJ peered down into her drink. "It could have happened to anyone, Sean."

"Then why is everyone talking about it?"

"Firefighters are gossiping old biddies. You know that." She put a hand on his shoulder. "Look, I'm sorry I even brought it up."

"Yeah, me too. Thanks for ruining my day." Sean tilted his head back and drank.

JJ, stung by Sean's response, started to get up to leave. Sean, feeling even worse now, reached out for her elbow. "I'm sorry. That was totally unnecessary. Sit back down. Please." He made himself look at her. " Do I really look that bad?"

"Yeah."

"Great."

"When was the last time you took a few days off, Sean? Got away on your own?"

"I don't know. Months ago."

"Maybe you should go away for a long weekend or something. It might help." JJ sighed. "I would love to get away on my own for a few days. Just to think."

"Why don't you?"

"Can't afford it. We're mortgaged up to the eyeballs on the house. Plus, Chris would probably squawk."

"So let him squawk." Out of the corner of his eye he saw Leary motioning to him. "Can you excuse me a minute?"

JJ nodded and Sean went to rejoin his friend. "What's up?"

"You hittin' on her?" Leary asked excitedly.

"What are you, out of your mind?"

"Why not? She's hot."

"She's also married. To a prick who carries a gun. Remember?"

"Oh, yeah, New York's finest. Forgot about that."

Sean poked him hard on the shoulder. "Here's an idea:

Why don't you mind your own business instead about worrying about everyone else's?"

Leary's mouth fell open. "What wild hair is up your ass today?"

"Nothing. Look, I gotta go. Give my best wishes to Nabby." He gave Leary a light, playful punch in the arm. "I'll catch you on the rebound, okay?"

He strode away. Everyone was getting on his nerves. Everything. JJ was right. He needed to get away.

"*Kiss her again* and she'll get a complex."

Gemma looked up from cuddling baby Domenica to see Michael and Theresa coming through the front door. Only twenty minutes earlier, they'd left to go out to dinner alone for the first time since their daughter was born. Now they were back, Theresa hurrying toward the couch with outstretched arms. Michael sounded like he was teasing but he looked alarmed.

"Is everything okay?" Gemma asked, surrendering the baby.

"You tell me." Michael sighed, regarding his wife affectionately. "Mama Bear couldn't relax. As soon as she ordered, she was convinced there'd been some catastrophe and we had to rush home."

Gemma eyed Theresa. "Thanks for the vote of confidence."

"It's not you," Theresa swore, kissing her daughter's plump fists. "It's some weird maternal thing. I couldn't bear to be away from her."

"You're away from her when you're at work," Michael pointed out.

"Only because I have to be. This is different."

"I can't wait 'til she goes away to college and you want to be her roommate," Michael teased.

"She's not going away to college. She's living at home and getting her degree online."

Crouching down, Michael put his mouth to his daughter's ear. "Your mama's *ubatz*, Domenica. The sooner you know it, the better."

Touched as she was by this domestic scene, Gemma felt out of place. "I guess my services aren't needed tonight."

"Don't go," Michael said. "We haven't had dinner yet." He gave Theresa a look. "We're going to order Chinese. Stay."

"You sure?"

"Stay," Theresa echoed. "I want to hear all about you and Sean."

"Actually," Gemma said, working hard to sound nonchalant, "Sean and I broke up."

Storm clouds brewed in Michael's eyes. "What happened?"

"It was mutual, Mikey. No need to spear him with your hockey stick."

"If you say so," Michael grumbled, heading toward the kitchen. "What do you people want to eat?"

"Eggplant in garlic sauce," Gemma called out.

"Moo shu pork," Theresa said. She turned to Gemma. "It was mutual?" she repeated, sounding unconvinced. Off in the kitchen, they could hear Michael opening and closing drawers, looking for the takeout menu.

"Kind of. I don't know."

As Theresa held her daughter on her lap, she and Domenica looked like a modern-day Madonna and Child. Both of them glowed with contentment, making Gemma painfully aware of the void in her own life. Gemma wanted what Theresa had: a husband, a baby, and a quiet Saturday night at home eating Chinese takeout and watching videos. Was that too much to ask?

"What happened?" Theresa demanded in a low voice tinged with urgency. Gemma took this as a sign they should have this discussion quickly, since Michael was now on the phone ordering their food.

"It just wasn't working," Gemma confessed sadly. "I was a wreck every time he went to work, which annoyed him, and my being a witch was a little too far off the beaten track for him. It was all sorts of things."

"What about the sex?" Theresa mouthed, as if the baby she now jostled on her knee might hear and understand.

Gemma blushed. "It was great. But he was involved in this bad fire a couple of weeks ago, and ever since then, it's been like talking to a brick wall."

"Maybe he was afraid that if he talked to you about it, you'd really freak out."

"Maybe."

It was possible Theresa had something there. Still, Sean's silence felt more symptomatic of a lack of trust, a failure to connect. Thinking about him, Gemma was overcome with remorse and self-doubt. Maybe she should have left him alone rather than prodding him to open up? But keeping your thoughts and feelings to yourself was so alien. Her family wore their hearts on their sleeves. She and Frankie talked everything to death. Communication was the yardstick by which you measured relationships: how intimately people knew each other's business. Now she wondered: Were there other ways of being intimate?

Michael reappeared in the living room. "Ten minutes on the chow. Which really means twenty." He settled down on the couch between his wife and cousin, transferring the baby onto his lap. "So, what did I miss?"

"Nothing," Theresa said.

He looked at Gemma, who detected sympathy in his eyes. "I can set you up with another of the guys on the team, if you want," he offered.

"I'll think about it." She held out her arms. "Give that baby back to me. You guys get to hold her all the time. I've got to steal time with her when I can."

Michael willingly obliged, handing Domenica over to Gemma. She was such an easygoing baby, affectionate, with a big, gummy smile for everyone. Holding her reminded Gemma of fiddling with a camera lens: It brought everything into sharp focus, including her own behavior. She should have cut Sean some slack. She should have waited for Sean to call her. He would have eventually; she knew that. She hated the way they parted, him snarling and angry, her just withdrawing. It felt wrong. She loved him. She wanted him. She would fight for him. If he needed some space, she'd give it to him. But there was no way she was going to give up on him, or let him give up on himself.

She waited until the next morning to pay Sean a visit. She had toyed with the idea of stopping by as soon as she got back from Michael and Theresa's, but it was late, and she had no idea of his schedule that week. Besides, she didn't want to look desperate. Or crazy.

It wasn't much of a peace offering, but Gemma had run out to battle the typical Sunday morning crowd to get coffee and some of the chocolate chip muffins Sean loved. Walking back to their building, she rehearsed what she'd say. *I come bearing muffins.* Too geeky. *Can we talk?* Better, more her style: simple, direct. Once he smelled the coffee and muffins, still warm in her hand, how could he resist? She wasn't feeling nervous, exactly. More anticipatory.

By the time she reached Sean's door, her heart was beating double time. She went to knock then hesitated, convinced she heard shouting coming from inside his apartment. Glancing around to make sure no one was looking, she quickly pressed her ear to the door. Definitely shouting, though it was muffled. Sounded like just one voice. Unsure of what to do, she stopped eavesdropping. If he was asleep and having a nightmare, ringing the be would wake him. If he was on the phone having an argument, she would interrupt him. *What to do?*

She bit her lip. The raised voice seemed to have gone quiet, at least momentarily. Meanwhile, the coffee in her hand was getting cold.

"To hell with it," she said out loud and rang the bell.

Immediately, Pete and Roger went crazy in their cages, their excited squawking louder than Gemma could have imagined. She cringed, praying Sean came to the door before his neighbors up and down the hall got angry. Ten-thirty on a Sunday morning might be too early for some people.

From within the apartment, footsteps pounded across the floor, and Gemma felt hope spring inside her. In just a few seconds, the door was going to open, and they'd be face-to-face. He'd smell the coffee and muffins, and break into that rugged smile that she loved, beckoning her inside. By the time the morning was through, everything would be worked out and they'd be back in each other's arms.

One lock clicked back. Gemma's stomach did a somersault.

Two more sprang back. Gemma held her breath.

Then the door opened, and everything fell apart.

Standing there wrapped in Sean's robe, her long blond hair shimmering wet from the shower, was a woman. She had a cell phone in her hand and a scowl stretched across her gorgeous face.

"Yes?" she asked impatiently. Behind her, the birds' squawking was deafening. "Shut the fuck up!" she yelled before her face seemed to collapse in on itself, from stress or annoyance, Gemma couldn't tell which.

"Um . . ."

"Sean's not here," the woman said curtly. From her clenched hand came the tinny sound of someone's voice shouting on the cell phone. "I'm sorry, I can't talk now."

She closed the door.

Gemma stood there, stunned. Who was that—? Were they—?

Gemma moved away from the door. *Sean and another woman.* She felt as though a giant invisible hand had plunged into her chest and torn her heart right out, leaving it hanging there, bruised and bloody. What a sap she'd been. Numb, she trudged back to the elevator. The sight of her own hallway drew tears as she remembered it strewn with stuffed animals, its emptiness now taunting her. How enchanted she'd been, willing to take a risk. Why had her intuition failed her?

Back in her own apartment, she made a beeline for the kitchen, throwing the coffee and muffins into the trash with gusto. She could still hear footsteps above—*boom! boom! boom!*—as the blond continued her fight with whomever was on the phone. Maybe it was Sean and they were having a lover's quarrel. *Good.* She hated her pettiness, but there it was. She didn't want to hate him, but she did. She hated them both. She slid into a kitchen chair, head in hands. Now what? The urge to wail, to just let it rip, was strong. Never, she vowed. Never again would she give her heart away so fast. If her faith had taught her anything, it was that things always happened for a reason, though the reason might not become clear for some time. There was a lesson in this, Gemma knew.

She just wished she knew what it was.

CHAPTER

14

After two days at the Blackfriar Inn, Sean had had enough. Walking through the woods, reveling in the scent of pine as shifting rays of sunshine dappled through the branches of the bare trees, his mind had returned again and again to the fire scene. He couldn't escape the boy in the hope chest. As he headed out for a final amble through the woods before going home, his thoughts turned to JJ. He'd called once to thank her for agreeing to bird-sit. It had been the perfect barter: JJ got a weekend away free of charge, and he got to go away without freaking out Roger and Pete.

He inhaled deeply, letting the crisp air fill his lungs. At least the weekend gave him space to think about Gemma. Their timing had been off from the beginning. Then there were her friends. And the witchcraft. Part of him envied her freedom to be completely who she was, convention be damned, open to the world. But that wasn't who he was. A fantasy flashed through his mind. He was apologizing to her for the way things had ended. "I hope we can still be friends," he heard himself saying. He burst into bitter laughter, the sound booming through the still woods, scattering a flock of starlings. He remembered a woman saying that to him and thinking, "Fuck you! You just wrecked my life and you have the gall to think I want to keep you as a friend? Screw you!"

But he did want Gemma to remain his friend.

Being with her was like opening a new book by your favorite author: You weren't quite sure what was in store, but you knew you'd like it. She was full of mystery and surprise, as sweet as she was iconoclastic. But he was toxic. As much as he yearned to maintain some kind of contact, he knew he shouldn't. Gemma deserved better than being dragged down with him into his black hole. He walked on, dead leaves crunching beneath his feet. Her last words to him had been unselfish, asking him to please take care of himself. He closed his eyes, sending a message to her. *I'm trying, Gemma, in the only way I know how. Please forgive me.*

He couldn't blame her if she didn't. He couldn't blame her for anything.

Turning the corner onto his street, Sean tensed as it dawned on him he might run into Gemma—if not today, then some other time. The thought made him sad, mainly because he could so vividly picture his own inept reaction to such an encounter: shuffling feet, muttered phrases. He sucked at post-relationship stuff.

Approaching his building, he noticed what looked like a bulging, fractured rainbow wrapped in plastic. Coming closer, he saw it was the menagerie of stuffed animals he'd bought for Gemma. She had put them out in the garbage, a clear message. He tore open the bag, rescuing the hot pink wildebeest. He wasn't sure why, only that it disturbed him to see that particular item carelessly tossed away. He'd give it to one of his nieces the next time he was out on Long Island.

Deflated, he entered the lobby and went up to his apartment. This was not how he'd wanted his day to begin.

Letting himself in, he noticed immediately that things were pretty much the way he'd left them—only cleaner. The rug was shampooed and vacuumed, windows denuded of grime, and nary a speck of dust could be seen on any surface.

"Merry Maids were here, I see," Sean teased, throwing his bag down and closing the door behind him. JJ's smile was friendly. At least someone was glad to see him.

"I couldn't help myself," JJ confessed, eyes momentarily straying to the TV, where she appeared to be watching some kind of canine competition on *Animal Planet*. "I get some of my best thinking done with a dust rag in my hand. How 'bout you? How was your weekend away?"

"I'm back early. What does that tell you?"

Pete and Roger were going nuts at the sight of him. Crossing the room, he released them from their cages, watching as they joyously winged around the room, reveling in their freedom. Most women screamed when he freed his birds, but JJ seemed unfazed. *How would Gemma have reacted?* he caught himself wondering. He shook his head, clearing his mind.

"So, what did you do for fun?" he asked.

"Went shopping. Cleaned. Mainly relaxed and did some thinking." Her eyes finally caught sight of the stuffed animal sitting by the doorway, and she looked at Sean questioningly.

"It's for one of my nieces. Go on: What else did you do?"

"That's it, really. You?"

"Hiked. Ate. Thought. Didn't sleep."

"We're quite a pair." Pointing the remote at the TV, she turned it off. "I can't tell you how grateful I am to you for letting me use your apartment this weekend, Sean. It really helped me clear my head."

"Hey, I got a free bird-sitter out of the deal, so we both benefited." He knew it was impolite, but he found himself hoping she'd leave soon. He wanted to be alone.

JJ rose from the couch, yawning. "I guess I should get going."

Thank you, Lord.

"Here, I'll walk you downstairs."

Throwing his jacket back on, he picked up her suitcase, quiet as she followed him out to the elevator.

"You know, anytime you want to talk—or anything—I'm here," JJ stuttered awkwardly.

"You, too," Sean managed.

"You're a good friend, Sean. I hate to see you feeling so sad."

Sean could feel his left temple pulsing. "You're a good friend, too, JJ. But I'm fine."

Isn't this better than sitting in your apartment crying? Gemma asked herself as she pedaled home from a bike ride around Central Park. It had been less than twenty-four hours since she'd knocked on Sean's door and had been kicked in the teeth, and she was still feeling pretty low. But Mother Nature's amazing restorative powers helped, and for that she was grateful.

Unlike some New Yorkers, Gemma didn't stash her bike away when the weather turned cold. She enjoyed riding in the fall and winter. There was something invigorating about bundling up on a cold morning and feeling the wind slap you awake. Gliding onto her street, she was brought up short: There, beneath the awning of her building, stood Sean and the willowy blond she'd seen in his bathrobe. She hit the breaks, squealing to a complete stop. They were talking animatedly, a smile lighting Sean's face as he turned back to say something to Tommy, the doorman. She kept watching, unable to help herself. Sean hailed a cab. And before the woman slipped inside, Sean drew her into an embrace.

Gemma froze, all feelings of well-being gone.

Here she'd had a lovely morning, had done something nice for herself, and how had the Goddess rewarded her? By smacking her upside the head with a vision from her own personal hell! Feeling sick, she turned her bike around and quickly pedaled off in the other direction. She would go to Frankie's.

"**Are you pulling** my pistol? He's screwing someone who looks like Malibu Barbie?"

Gemma nodded.

"That's pretty fast if you ask me. He must have been nobbing her all along."

Gemma grimaced, hating Frankie's penchant for brutal truth. Phrased that way, it made her relationship with Sean sound insignificant, a mere blip on the radar screen of his life. She watched as Frankie tried to bluff her way through making some grilled cheese sandwiches. Many of the tasks of daily living seemed to elude Frankie, including food prep. Gemma had no doubt her friend would subsist completely on Diet Coke, cigarettes, and Balance bars if she could get away with it.

Frankie awkwardly turned the sandwiches in the frying pan. "Shit—why is the butter smoking?"

"Turn down the heat."

"Here, you cook it."

They switched places, Gemma relieving Frankie of her spatula. "Maybe I should move," Gemma muttered.

"What are you, nuts? You're living in a great apartment in a great building and you're paying peanuts for it!"

"Yeah, but—"

" 'I don't know if I can handle running into them,' "
Frankie mimicked, knowing exactly what Gemma was
going to say.

"Bingo."

"Screw him," Frankie railed. "Don't let him drive you
out! Don't let him win."

"It's not a war, Frankie."

"Well, it should be! Goddamn asshole hurts my best
friend? He deserves death." She sidled up to Gemma at the
stove. "Can't you put a spell on him? Make sure that every
cab he hails for the rest of his life passes him by or something?"

"I would never do that." She pressed down on one of
the sandwiches with the spatula. "Though it is tempting."

"So, what happens now?"

"Business as usual, I guess, with the added bonus of
hoping I don't run into them. And worrying about my
grandmother."

"Yeah, what's up with that?"

"Michael's working on getting her an appointment with
one of the top geriatricians in the city. She's forgetful,
moody . . ."

"Maybe it's PMS," Frankie joked.

"I wish."

"Keep me posted, okay?"

Gemma nodded, while Frankie went to the fridge.
"Know what I think you should do about Sean?" she
asked, pulling out a carton of milk.

"What?"

"Kill him."

Gemma laughed.

"No, seriously. Hire a hit man. I bet you anything your
cousin Anthony knows some people who know some people. Take him out. Smoke him. Arrange for him to sleep
with the fishes. Put a cap in his ass."

"You're nuts, you know that?"

"Yeah, but I made you laugh, didn't I?"

"True."

"So, any movement on the Uther front?" Frankie asked casually as she took a slug of milk directly from the carton, then put it back.

"I'll do it this week, I promise. It'll give me something happy to focus on." Gemma mulled this over as she slid the crisp, golden sandwiches onto two waiting plates. Playing Cupid's assistant always made her feel better. It would help take her mind off things. "What do you want me to do if he says he's not interested?"

"He won't," Lady Midnight replied.

"I never got to ask you: How did your Battle of Hastings reenactment go?"

Gemma handed Uther a cup of chamomile tea, sliding back onto the stool beside his. Half an hour into tarot lessons she always took a brief ten-minute break, having learned over the years that most people's attention span couldn't last a solid hour. Uther was the exhausting exception, but she took the break anyway. Her goal was to slip Frankie's phone number into his hand by the time the ten minutes were up.

Uther looked so pleased to be asked about his reenactment it almost broke Gemma's heart. "It was fantastic," he raved. "I was part of King Harold's shield wall. I had to pretend to get hit in the eye with an arrow."

"Wow. That must have been . . . painful."

"Painful but rewarding." Uther sipped his tea. "We might tackle the Battle of Agincourt this summer."

"Sounds great."

"You should come to a meeting sometime." He gave a small pause. "You and your friend."

Gemma smiled slyly. "You liked her, didn't you?"

"Lady Midnight? Ho ho, I should say so."

"Her name is Frankie. Lady Midnight is her on-air personality." *Confuse the two and you're doomed.* "She thought you were cute." *In a Renaissance Fair kind of way.*

"Really." Uther puffed up with pride. "I found the damsel rather alluring myself."

You should see her with her eye patch on, thought Gemma. How perfect were these two for each other, Frankie with her patch, Uther running around the park in chain mail pretending to be hit in the eye with an arrow?

"Would you like her phone number?"

Uther turned guarded. "Phone number?"

"Yes. To call her. So the two of you can get together?" *I know you'd prefer writing her a note on parchment and putting it in a raven's beak, but this is the twenty-first century, Uth.*

"Are you giving it to me of your own volition or did she say you could give it to me?"

"She said I could give it to you," said Gemma, feeling like she'd taken a time machine back to seventh grade. What next? Would he ask her to ask Frankie to meet him by his locker after necromancy practice?

"I'll take it, then. Are you sure you're all right with this?"

Gemma did a double take. "Why wouldn't I be?"

"I feel you and I have a connection that seems to go beyond this world, sweet lady, and I wouldn't want to upset you," said Uther as he attempted to peer at her seductively over the rim of his mug.

"Uther, I have a boyfriend," Gemma lied. There was no way she was going to let him know she was available. Not when he was talking about otherworldly connections, whatever that meant.

"Oh yes, him." Uther looked displeased. "You mentioned him at the street fair. What is his trade?"

Her temptation was to answer, "None of your business," but since she was trying to grease the wheels of romance for Frankie, she felt she had no choice but to be chatty and amiable.

"He's a firefighter, but he used to be a stockbroker."

As soon as the words were out, Gemma thought: *Sean's right. Why do I do that? Use his past profession as some sort of qualifier, as if what he does now might not be enough?*

Uther looked impressed. "A very noble profession indeed. When you think about it, he's a dragon slayer of sorts."

"Yes." Time to steer the conversation away from Sean. "Here, I'll write Frankie's number for you." She grabbed one of her business cards from the seashell by the register and jotted her friend's number down on the back. "As you already know"—she flashed him a smile—"Frankie is on the air from midnight to six during the week. The best time to call her is usually after two in the afternoon."

"Thank you, sweet lady. I shall call her anon—or not anon exactly, but on the morrow." He looked at the card before slipping it into his pocket. "One quick question: Is she Pagan?"

"She's undecided. She believes in the trinity, but in her case it's Aerosmith, the Beatles, and Led Zeppelin."

Uther seemed amused by this, and smiled. "Fascinating."

"I agree. Let's get back to our tarot, shall we?"

CHAPTER

15

"I'm trying to decide which I hate you for more," Gemma told Michael as they met up in Dante's parking lot and began strolling toward the restaurant. "Setting me up with another crazy hockey player, or not calling me when you got the geriatrician appointment for Nonna."

"I didn't call because there was no way you could have come," Michael said, holding the door open for her. "It was in the middle of the day in the middle of the week."

"Plus my mother didn't want me there, right?"

Michael was silent.

"I knew it."

"As for Boris," Michael continued, changing the subject, "I asked if you wanted me to set you up with another nice guy on the team, and you said yes."

"He took out his teeth over dessert, Michael. Said he felt comfortable with me."

Michael cringed. "But he was nice, right?"

"I don't know! Maybe! I was focused on trying not to stare at his gums."

Michael looked surprised. "What happened to my sweet, open-minded cousin who feels love and compassion for all God's creatures?"

"She got burned by a firefighter. Next question, please."

Entering the banquet room where the rest of the extended family were gathered, Gemma detected a wave of tension ripple through the room. She'd been a witch for years; you'd think they would get over it by now. But no: All she had to do was show up and some of her family acted as if Satan had materialized. It was disheartening, not to mention tiresome.

All morning, as a way to cope, Gemma had changed the words of a song from *The Sound of Music* and had been singing, "How do we solve a problem like Nonna Maria?" Nonna was the reason everyone was here: She'd been diagnosed with middle-stage Alzheimer's disease. Living alone was no longer an option.

"I hope this isn't too awful," Michael confided as they sat down at the long, extended table with the rest of the family.

Gemma took in the sea of familiar faces surrounding her. Everyone she expected to be present was there: her own mother, her Aunt Millie, Theresa, Anthony and his wife Angie, assorted cousins and their spouses. Her eye caught her mother's, and for a split second, it almost seemed as if her mother might acknowledge her, maybe even smile. But the moment passed as Gemma's mother pointedly turned her body to talk to Aunt Millie. Gemma had become a pro at shaking off such blatant rejection, but deep down, it still hurt. She turned to Anthony, seated to her left.

"Where's Aunt Betty Anne?"

"Home taking care of Nonna," he answered glumly before squeezing her arm. "Glad you came, Gem. Ignore the *faccia brutas* who won't give you the time of day."

Gemma smiled, touched, since it wasn't too long ago Anthony was among them himself. "Thanks, Ant."

"All right, everybody, let's get down to business," Michael said, clapping his hands briskly to get everyone's attention. Gemma stole a sidelong glance at Anthony; he was rolling his eyes, his lifelong annoyance at Michael's tendency to take control evident. Amazing how some things never changed. The two of them would be in their nineties and they would still be rubbing each other the wrong way.

"As you know," Michael began, "last week Theresa, along with Aunt Connie and Aunt Millie, took Nonna to a geriatrician. After giving her a bunch of tests, the doctor determined it was Alzheimer's."

"What kind of tests?" asked cousin Paulie, who'd come in all the way from Commack.

Michael looked to Theresa.

"Memory tests, language tests, you name it. There's something called the seven-minute screen that doctors use to check for Alzheimer's, since there's no one test for the disease, *per se*. Nonna didn't do very well."

"Tell 'em straight," Aunt Millie croaked, sucking on her Winston. "She couldn't tell a friggin' banana from an orange. Didn't know what year it was. The doctor told her to draw a clock with hands pointed at quarter to three and she couldn't do it. It was awful."

Paulie thrust his head forward, squinting with disbelief. "They ask you to draw fruit and that's how they tell if you're senile?"

"Senility is different than Alzheimer's," Theresa said patiently. "Believe me, Paulie, this doctor knows what he's doing. He's one of the top geriatricians in the city. If he says Nonna has Alzheimer's, Nonna has Alzheimer's."

"Shit," Paulie muttered. "Poor Nonna."

"So, what do we do?" Anthony demanded.

Theresa sighed. "Well, they want to put her on drugs

to help slow the progress of it, so that's one good thing."
She looked distraught. "But there's no cure for
Alzheimer's. It just gets worse and worse. In the meantime, Nonna's reached the stage where it's dangerous to
leave her alone."

Leaden silence followed as the family contemplated
this. Then Anthony's wife Angie spoke up.

"I guess we gotta put her in a home."

Anthony groaned, a dead giveaway that his wife had
put her foot in her mouth. Closing her eyes, Gemma
quickly envisioned a protective blue light around Angie.
She was going to need it. Gemma opened her eyes just in
time to see her own mother glaring at Angie from across
the table.

"Did you just say what I think you said?" Connie Dante
asked.

"Ma," Gemma warned.

"You keep out of this," her mother commanded sharply.
Her eyes flicked back to Angie contemptuously. "Did you,
who weren't even born into this family, suggest putting my
mother away like she was a piece of furniture going to a
warehouse?"

Gemma's heart went out to Angie as she struggled to
put things right. "I didn't mean to suggest—"

"Where you from, hon?" Aunt Millie cut in.

Angie blinked in confusion, her face turning red. "I
don't—"

"She means where are your people from," Gemma's
mother clarified as she drummed her pointy purple finger-
nails on the tabletop.

"Oh. Como."

Gemma's mother and Aunt exchanged knowing
glances, as if geography determined behavior. Her
mother's voice was patronizing as she addressed Angie.
"We're Sicilian, hon. Maybe in the North families throw

out the elderly like an old pair of boots, but not in the South. Sicilians care for their elderly."

"North, south, what is this, the friggin' Civil War here?" Anthony asked plaintively. "Let's focus on what we're gonna do." He put a protective arm around Angie's shoulder. Gemma was glad to see it.

"Well, we're sure as shit not putting her in a nursing home," cousin Paulie declared, looking around the room nervously to make sure he wasn't doing something radical, like expressing his own opinion.

"Then what are we going to do?" Theresa demanded. "Angie's suggestion wasn't out of line."

Aunt Millie shook her head disgustedly as she stubbed out her cigarette. "Another one with the nursing home."

"I'm not saying we should put her in a nursing home," Theresa said sharply. "I'm asking what the alternative is."

"Taking care of her at home," Michael said as if it were the most obvious thing in the world.

"Who, Mikey?" Gemma prodded gently. "Are we hiring home health aides? What?"

Cousin Paulie looked horrified. "I can't afford to chip in for some nurse. I'm barely making ends meet as it is."

"Maybe if you stopped buying a new car every freaking year, you'd save money," Anthony observed.

Paulie half rose out of his seat. *"Vaffancul!"*

"Whoa, everyone, come on, settle down," Michael pleaded. "This is a serious problem here. We need to take care of it."

"You're just jealous," Paulie jeered at Anthony.

"Yeah, right, I wish I could buy a guineamobile—"

"Cut the shit, Anthony!" Michael snapped. Anthony and Paulie settled back in their chairs, glowering at each other.

"I don't want some stranger taking care of my mother," Gemma's mother declared.

"Amen," Aunt Millie agreed, lighting up as she turned

to regard her sister. "Remember Mrs. DiNuova, used to live on Seventh Avenue?"

Gemma's mother nodded fearfully.

"Well, her mother got sick and they hired some Dominican nurse to take care of her. By the time the old lady died, all the Hummel figures were gone from the house."

"I hear there's a huge market for Hummels in the Dominican Republic," Michael said drily.

"Don't make fun," Aunt Millie rasped, shaking a finger at him across the table. "It's true."

"So, if neither of you want 'some stranger' to take care of your mother, does that mean you're going to do it?" Gemma asked.

The family looked at her mother and Aunt Millie expectantly. Gemma almost felt sorry for them: They looked like two aging deer trapped in headlights.

"I'll do it part of the time," Gemma's mother conceded reluctantly.

"Me, too," said Aunt Millie, blowing smoke out of the side of her mouth. "And so will Betty Anne."

"Let's nail this down," Michael insisted. "Because if we're going to do this, we have to start right away. Today."

Gemma's mother heaved a world-weary sigh. "I can watch her during the day on Monday, Tuesday, and Wednesday."

"I'll do Thursday and Friday," Aunt Millie offered.

"What about weekends?"

The room went silent.

Gemma ran through her own schedule in her head. "I can do Sundays," she offered tentatively.

"I don't think that's a very good idea," a voice piped up. It belonged to her cousin Sharmaine, Paulie's sister. Gemma and Sharmaine had never gotten along. Once Gemma revealed she was a witch, she became *persona non grata* to the holier-than-thou Sharmaine, who, ironically, was rumored to be banging her parish priest on a regular basis.

"What's your beef?" Michael asked politely.

"You know what my beef is," Sharmaine sniffed, staring disdainfully at Gemma. "I don't think it's a very good idea for her to spend too much time around Nonna. That witch crap might upset her."

Gemma went to open her mouth but a quick look from Michael told her that, as family facilitator, he preferred to handle it. That was fine with Gemma.

"Are you saying you'll watch Nonna on Sundays, Sharmaine?" Michael asked.

"I can't," Sharmaine said coolly. "I'm busy."

"Doing what?" Anthony chortled. "Letting Father Flynn slip you his special communion wafer?"

"Bite my ass, Anthony," Sharmaine snapped.

"Just one bite?" Anthony lobbed back. "Two or three might help make it smaller."

"You sonofa—"

"Stop!" Gemma shouted. Sometimes she wondered why she still gave a damn about being accepted in her family, especially when they behaved like sniping, backbiting lunatics. She knew it happened in lots of families, but hers seemed to have elevated it to an art. "Can we please stop tearing each other to pieces and focus on the problem at hand?" Her family's gaze bordered on the mutinous, but she'd made her point. She turned to Michael. "You were saying?"

"You sure you can be at Nonna's on Sundays?"

Gemma nodded. "Yes. I can do all day Sunday and Sunday night, and probably Monday and Wednesday nights as well. I just need to check with my part-timer."

Michael looked around the room, his gaze pointedly resting on Sharmaine. "Can anyone else help out?"

Sharmaine suddenly became fascinated by her own feet.

"If Connie does some, I do some, and Gemma does some, Betty Anne can do the rest," Aunt Millie said. "She doesn't have a job."

"She'll kill you if it means missing bingo," Gemma's mother pointed out.

"Let her try," Millie growled.

Gemma thought the matter settled, but Michael's uneasy expression said otherwise. "Are you sure about this?" he asked her again. "With the exception of Paulie, everyone here lives in Brooklyn. You sure you don't mind jackassing out from the city?"

"It's not a problem," Gemma assured him. "Besides," she added with a hint of self-deprecation, "I have no life anyway."

"Plus broomsticks are faster than public transportation," Anthony kidded her under his breath, winking as he nudged her in the ribs.

"You're an idiot, you know that?" Gemma murmured back.

"An idiot who gives you free cannolis all the time, so watch it."

"That settles it, then," Michael said. "Nonna will be watched at home by Aunt Connie, Aunt Millie, Aunt Betty Anne, and Gemma."

"Depending upon what shifts I'm working, I can be a backup person," Angie offered.

"Me, too," Theresa put in.

"We've got it covered then," Michael said, looking relieved. "Meeting over. Everyone *mangia*."

Moving toward the buffet table where Anthony had set up steaming trays of lasagna, Gemma was suddenly hit with a profound sense of exhaustion. Though the family meeting had lasted less than an hour, the emotional pitch had left her drained. Or maybe she was feeling drained by the prospect of shuttling back and forth between Manhattan and Bensonhurst? She didn't doubt she could help to take care of her grandmother while still running her store, nor was she having second thoughts. She *was* a little worried about where all her energy would come from.

She had just scooped out a helping of lasagna when she felt a light tap on her shoulder. She turned. Her mother was there.

"Hi, Ma," she said, instinctively tensing. Her reaction to her mother had become Pavlovian by now, her body bracing for rejection and stress. "What's up?"

"Thank you for offering to help take care of your grandmother," she said stiffly.

"I love Nonna. You know that."

"Yes, well, it's very nice of you," her mother continued, not quite looking at her. With nothing more to say, she moved to join Aunt Millie at a nearby table. Gemma stared after her, touched. Her mother had never been one for compliments, even before they were estranged. For her to say something nice was monumental. Elated, Gemma turned back to the buffet table. Perhaps something positive would come out of Nonna's illness. She certainly hoped so.

"*Let me just* say one thing: You're out of your fucking mind."

Frankie's voice was so loud that Gemma sank down in her seat as the other patrons in the diner turned to look at them. It was bad enough Frankie had come strolling through the door with a neck brace on, drawing attention to herself. Did she have to bellow on top of it?

"Keep it down, will you, please?"

"How on earth are you going to run your store *and* help take care of your grandmother?"

"I can do it."

"How? No wait, let me guess: Your magickal powers enable you to practice bilocation."

"I wish."

"Seriously, Gem, how are you going to manage this? You'll be so exhausted you won't have time for a life."

"What life do I have now?"

"That's not the point," Frankie insisted. "You and I both know why you offered to do this."

Gemma shifted uneasily. "Oh? Why's that?"

"Because you want to get back in your mother's good graces."

Gemma took a sip of coffee. "That's part of it." There was no denying it: She had come to the same realization a few days before, sitting at her kitchen table loading her new insane schedule on to her Palm Pilot, envisioning months, maybe even years, of sheer bloody exhaustion. Then it hit her: Part of her reason for doing it was because maybe—just maybe—it would somehow help redeem her in the eyes of her family, especially her mother.

"You don't understand. My mother came up to me after the meeting and actually thanked me for offering to help. That's major, Frankie."

"No, it's sad. I hate seeing you scraping and bowing when Queen Connie decides to throw you a few crumbs."

"Better crumbs than nothing." She appreciated Frankie's protectiveness toward her, but in this case, Frankie was missing the point. Her mother had to start somewhere. One crumb, however miniscule, was a step in the right direction.

Frankie frowned. "I still think you're nuts to take this on."

"I love my grandmother, Frankie," Gemma replied softly. "I want to spend as much time with her as possible before"—she began choking up—"she doesn't know who I am anymore."

"Oh, Gem." Digging into the Beatles lunchbox she used

as a purse, Frankie pulled out a minipack of tissues, handing them across the table. "That's really sweet."

"I guess." Gemma dabbed at her eyes.

"No, it is. Nonna's lucky to have you. Really."

"Please shut up before you make me sob," Gemma joked, but she wasn't kidding. One more tender word about how nice she was being to her Nonna and the waterworks would commence in full. That would really endear them to the surrounding diners.

Since Frankie rarely beat around the bush, Gemma thought she'd return the favor. "What happened to your neck?"

"I think I ruptured a disk."

"How?"

"Playing frisbee with Alice Cooper."

"Why don't you go to a doctor and find out for sure?"

Frankie mumbled something about insurance, and Gemma let it go. How did people at the radio station, people who might not know and love Frankie the way she did, react to this never-ending parade of afflictions and illnesses? "Don't you worry about being perceived as sickly by your bosses?" Gemma asked. "Isn't it a liability?"

"It's not my fault my immune system is suppressed and I'm unlucky," Frankie replied indignantly. "Besides, I rarely ever miss work. Ever. As long as Lady Midnight sounds great behind the mike, who cares if her body is falling apart?"

But it's not. You just think it is. Or want it to be. Or something.

"Speaking of Lady Midnight, did you ever hear from Uther?" Gemma asked.

She couldn't believe it: Frankie, who'd probably spent the night with more rock stars than Pamela des Barres, looked almost bashful. "I did."

"And—?"

"We're going out for a goblet of mead on Saturday night."

"That's great!" She was happy for Frankie. For Uther, too. Maybe this would help Frankie get over her loser ex-husband. "Your neck should be okay by then, right?"

"I hope so." Unable to move just her head because of the brace, Frankie craned her entire torso around, looking for Stavros. "Where's the man with the coffeepot when you need him?"

"I'm sure he'll be along in a minute."

"Speaking of men," Frankie said as she stiffly turned back to face Gemma, "have you run into Sean?"

"No, thank God. I'm sure he and Barbie have been holed up in his apartment having fun."

"Torturing ourselves again, are we?"

"Not torture," Gemma replied calmly. "Just fact."

She was grateful when Stavros interrupted them, making a big fuss out of Frankie's injury and giving them a blow-by-blow account of his recent hernia operation. Sean Kennealy wasn't a subject on which she wanted to dwell.

This time, Sean thought, crawling on his hands and knees through smoke so thick he couldn't make out his own hand in front of him, *I am not going to leave anyone behind.* Having already checked one bedroom and finding no one, he'd moved on to the next, and the next, always with the same feverish tape loop running through his brain: *Check the closet. Check under the bed. Check the furniture. Check everywhere you have to.*

Swinging his ax in front of him, he hit something solid, and felt for it. Bed. Raising himself up on his knees, he patted the top of the mattress. Empty. Move on.

Feeling his way, he came to another door, and felt for the handle. It seemed stuck. Jostling it, he heard the piercing warning bell go off on his breathing pack. He had five minutes of air left and then he'd have to get the hell out. Shit. He gave the door handle one good turn, and it seemed to do the trick. Proud of his determination, he flung the door open wide.

The boy stood smiling at him, glowing green in the jungle of his mother's wardrobe. "Why didn't you find me last time?" he asked Sean. Sean scooped him up into his arms and started crawling toward the bedroom door. But just as he reached it, the door slammed shut in his face. Then he woke up.

"Sean?"

Sean looked up from his dad's La-Z-Boy to see his mother shuffling into the living room. She'd been complaining about not seeing enough of him, so he'd decided to go home to Oceanside for the weekend. "You okay?" she asked.

"I'm fine. Go back to bed. It's the middle of the night."

"I could say the same to you," she pointed out. "What's going on? I heard you rattling around in the kitchen before."

"I was just getting some milk. I'm sorry. I didn't mean to wake you."

"I was awake anyway," his mother yawned, gathering the folds of her bathrobe around her as she sat down on the couch.

"Oh, yeah?" Sean found it amusing they were both up treading the boards at 3 A.M. He'd forgotten his mother was an insomniac. He had strong childhood memories of waking up to pee in the middle of the night and there she'd be in the living room, staring into the flickering blue light of the TV screen. "What's eating you?"

"Life," his mother replied.

Sean chuckled. "You and me both."

"Everything okay with you and Gemma?"

"Great," Sean lied. He didn't want to have this discussion with his mother at three in the morning.

"I like her," his mother said thoughtfully. "She's very genuine, down to earth. Pretty, too."

Sean forced himself to smile. "I'll tell her you said so."

His mother reached out, putting a hand on his knee. "You sure you're all right? You forget: I'm a mother, which means I've got a built-in bullshit detector. What's going on?"

Sean shrugged. "Just, you know"—he coughed nervously as the feeling of his throat closing up suddenly seized him, and he realized he might cry—"work stuff. Bad dreams about work."

His mother reached out to touch his cheek. "Talk to me, honey. C'mon."

"Uh, no, I really can't."

"Sean—"

"I almost let a kid die, Mom," he blurted out, unable to hold it in any longer. "There was a fire and I fucked up and I almost let a kid die." He felt haunted as he stared into his mother's eyes. "Ever since then I can't stop thinking about him. I see him everywhere."

"Oh, Seany." His mother gathered him up into her arms as if he were still her little boy. "It's okay."

"It's not okay!" Sean replied hoarsely. "Part of my job is to be thorough and I failed, I failed that little boy—" He broke off, sobs shaking his shoulders as he covered his face with his hands. "Oh, Christ."

It felt good to cry. What was the word? *Cathartic.* Though a rogue thought kept appearing as his mother soothed him and held him tight: *I wish it was Gemma I was talking to. I wish it was Gemma holding me tight. Fuck, I miss her.*

Eventually, he pulled himself together and pulled away.

"Sorry about that," he said gruffly, embarrassed at having lost control.

"Don't be ridiculous. What you're experiencing is very, very common. Your father used to react the same way."

"Yeah?" It made him feel a little better to hear that.

"Absolutely."

He pressed his fingertips against his eye sockets. "I'm so tired. But I'm afraid if I go back to sleep . . ."

"I think you might need to talk to someone about this," his mother suggested, sounding like she was walking on eggshells.

"Yeah, I know," Sean admitted miserably. "But it's not my way, you know, talking things to death."

"But this is affecting your life, Sean."

"I know." Guilt descended on him as his mind flashed back to the last time he'd seen Gemma. She'd said the same thing, and he'd cut her off at the knees. Now he saw that she wasn't pushing, wasn't prying, wasn't trying to make him into something he wasn't. Like his mother, she simply saw someone she loved in pain and wanted to do whatever she could to alleviate it. What a clueless jerk he was.

"They have therapists at the fire department now," his mother continued carefully. "Maybe you should check it out."

"I might, Ma. Thanks."

Much to his chagrin, he found himself still dogged by embarrassment. The guys at the house kept their mouths shut when they needed help. Was he being weak because he was unable to suck it up and take it "like a man"? Then he asked himself, where had that attitude gotten his father? He remembered the awful, stomach-churning feeling of coming home from school not knowing what mood his father would be in, and he knew he had to talk this out no matter how uncomfortable it made him. Exhaustion suddenly swallowed him up, making him feel muzzy-headed

He hadn't been exaggerating when he'd told his mother he had qualms about going back to sleep. But now that he'd spilled his guts, maybe sleep would come, and he could rest. He appreciated that she'd listened to him and hadn't passed judgment. She was a good mother; he told her so and saw the pleasure in her eyes.

But he wished he'd been comforted by Gemma.

CHAPTER

16

The last time Gemma had slept over at her grandmother's house, she'd been twenty, seeking solace after a particularly bad fight with her mother. They'd stayed up late into the night talking, Gemma wishing Nonna were her mother. When she was small, she used to sleep over all the time, the sound of Nonna's snoring up the hall a comfort to her. Gemma smiled, remembering the pure joy of sitting at the kitchen table, legs swinging, while Nonna made ricotta pancakes. Afterward they'd go to church, and Gemma would be entranced by the multicolored shafts of sunlight filtering through the stained glass windows. Nonna said sunbeams were God's fingers reaching down to touch the earth. Gemma found that a comfort, too.

Now, pulling up in front of Nonna's house on a Sunday morning, she was surprised she felt nervous about the day and night ahead. Gemma knew she must be conscious of not behaving differently toward her grandmother, unless she needed to for Nonna's own safety. Yes, a definite diagnosis of Alzheimer's had been made, but Nonna was still the same person, and deserved to be treated with the same love and respect, not like a child or some doddering old woman. She prayed everyone else in the family was on the same page.

The door was opened by her cousin Anthony, who had insisted on continuing his tradition of taking Nonna to early Mass at St. Finbar's.

"How ya' doin?" he asked, leaning in for a quick peck to the cheek. "Traffic okay?"

"At this hour, it was a breeze." Shrugging off her cape, Gemma shivered. "It's like an icebox in here."

"Nonna says she's hot."

"Where is she?"

"In the kitchen having her traditional post-Mass snack: espresso and *sfogliatelle*." Anthony reached for his coat, draped over the back of the easy chair. "She did good in church: knew where she was, didn't want to get up and wander around." He chuckled. "She didn't know who Father Clementine was, though. She leans over to me and says really loud, 'Who's that fat bastard?' "

Gemma laughed appreciatively. "I'm sorry I missed that."

"Bella?"

"In here, Nonna, talking to Anthony," Gemma called in the direction of the kitchen. "I'll be in in a minute."

"You need anything?" Anthony asked, turning up his collar.

"I'm fine."

"Okay, then, I'm gonna take off. I'll be at the restaurant around noon if you need me. Ange is on duty today. Mikey's in Pittsburgh, but I think Theresa's home if you need help or anything. Just give a shout."

"Maybe I'll give Sharmaine a call," Gemma joked.

"Putan'," Anthony growled under his breath. "I never liked that one."

"You and me both. Take care, Ant," she said as she

watched him plod down Nonna's steps and up the street. Michael was a bounder, Anthony a plodder. What was she?

"Bella, I'm so happy you decided to visit." Nonna's face flushed with pleasure as she looked up from the kitchen table. "Can you stay for lunch?"

"Lunch, dinner, the whole shebang!"

No sooner had the words slipped out of her mouth than Nonna's visage darkened. "In, out, in, out, all these people trooping through my house. What the hell is going on? Can't an old woman live in peace?"

Same old Nonna. Speak the truth. "You don't have a choice, Non," Gemma explained gently. "Remember when you went to see the doctor with Mom and Aunt Millie?"

Nonna looked suspicious.

"Well, the doctor said you shouldn't be alone anymore. That's why we've all been here. We're keeping you company, making sure you don't get hurt."

"I can take care of myself," Nonna muttered fiercely.

"I know you can. We're just here to help."

This seemed to pacify her. "All right."

Gemma slid into a chair next to her. "What would you like to do today?"

"I'd like to get out of my church clothes, for a start."

"Okay." Gemma hesitated. Should she let her grandmother go upstairs on her own to change, or should she go with her? One option courted the potential for injury, the other for insult. Gemma decided to be straightforward. "Would you like some help?"

"The company would be nice."

Gemma waited until her grandmother had finished her coffee, then followed her upstairs. She couldn't remember the last time she'd actually been in her grandmother's bedroom. It had to be when she was a very small child. She was shocked but not surprised to see nothing had changed.

The sagging double bed with the faded chenille bedspread was still there, and the walls were still adorned by pictures of saints, their beatific smiles rendered all the more mysterious by the glow of the votive candles atop Nonna's dresser that never seemed to go out or need replacing.

Those might have to go.

Her eye caught the set of rosary beads draped over one corner of the dresser mirror, and a cross made of palm fronds stuck into the corner of the other. As a little girl, she'd been frightened by the religious accoutrements of her grandmother's room, convinced the eyes of all the paintings were following her. But now she found comfort in their immutability, appreciating their value as symbols of a life richly lived in faith.

Sinking down on the bed, Nonna took off her shoes. She peeled off her stockings next before moving to her dresser to remove her jewelry.

"Want these?" she said to Gemma, holding up her earrings.

Gemma scrunched up her nose. "What?"

"Take them," Nonna urged. "I'd rather see you enjoy them while I'm still alive."

"Thank you." Gemma took the marcasite teardrops and slipped them into her pocket. She had no intention of keeping them, knowing that some members of her family would accuse her of starting to clean out Nonna's house while she was still alive. Besides, Nonna might not be fully aware of what she was doing. Tomorrow she might want to wear those very same earrings, and then what?

Sighing heavily, Nonna grabbed the hem of her skirt to pull her dress over her head. Gemma was initially shocked by the lumpy terrain of her grandmother's bare legs, the sagging flesh crosshatched with a network of varicose and spider veins. *This'll be me someday,* she thought, and her heart filled with tenderness. *This will be all of us.*

The dress was up around Nonna's neck now, covering her face.

"Help!" Nonna cried out, her voice muffled through the material. "I'm caught on something."

Alarmed, Gemma went to her aid. The crocheted neckline of Nonna's dress was snagged on a chain she wore around her neck. As delicately as she could, Gemma worked to untangle the two. That's when she saw it: The charm hanging from Nonna's necklace was the *cimaruta,* an ancient Pagan charm traditionally used to ward off the evil eye. She stared at it. In Italy, it was called "the witch charm." Its three main branches symbolized the goddess Diana in her three aspects as maiden, mother, and crone. Hanging from each branch were other symbols: a fish, a hand, a key, a crescent moon—each having a specific meaning.

"Nonna," Gemma asked as she helped her off with her dress, "where did you get the *cimaruta?*"

"Ah," said Nonna, fingering the beautiful silver charm. "You like it?"

"Where did you get it?" Gemma asked again. "How long have you had it?"

Nonna turned away, an almost imperceptible smile playing across her lips. "That's my secret."

Gemma's eyes were glued to her as she went to her closet to pull out a pair of slacks and a blouse. *She's a witch. I know it. I feel it!* The thought excited her. It meant the ancient ways were part of her birthright. She wasn't an oddball at all; this was in her blood! What would her mother have to say about that?

Nonna, meanwhile, had slipped into her slacks. But as her fingers went to the neck of her blouse, they hesitated, rubbing the button there. Gemma watched and waited. Maybe Nonna wanted to wear something else? Nonna looked down at the open blouse, then at Gemma, her face contorted with bafflement.

Oh, God. She can't remember how to do the buttons.

"Here, let me," Gemma said softly. Slowly, with great care, she buttoned the front of her grandmother's blouse. "Better?"

"Better," Nonna repeated, her relief obvious. She glanced at Gemma shyly. "Would you mind brushing my hair?"

"I would love to."

Steering Nonna to sit at her vanity, Gemma loosened the silver braid of her hair. Picking up the stiff horsehair brush Nonna had had for as long as she could remember, she began brushing. Nonna closed her eyes, seeming to lose herself in the luxurious sensation. When she opened them, her eyes met Gemma's in the vanity mirror.

"You and me," Nonna said. "We're a lot alike."

Gemma leaned over, lovingly pressing her own cheek against her grandmother's older, more papery version. "I know," Gemma whispered.

Sean hadn't been sure what to expect. He was pleasantly surprised to find the counseling unit looked like any other office, with out-of-date magazines littering the low coffee table in the waiting room, and furniture that had seen better days. He had an appointment to talk to Lieutenant Dan Murray, who had put in his twenty years of active service with the department and was now working as a full-time counselor. Sean liked him on sight: Bow-legged, pot-bellied, with a big, white handlebar mustache, he brought to mind a friendly, talking walrus.

Murray's tone was friendly but concerned. "What can I do for you, Sean?"

As briefly as he could, Sean explained what he'd been going through since the brownstone fire. Murray listened intently, giving the occasional encouraging nod. He seemed neither surprised nor shocked by what Sean told him, even when Sean related the details of how, walking down the street, he'd felt like he couldn't breathe after seeing a hope chest in the window of a furniture store.

"That's called a trigger," Murray explained. "Extremely common after a traumatic incident. Something visual, a certain smell, a sound—anything can bring you back to the fire scene and with it comes all those attendant feelings: guilt, pain, fear, you name it."

"Yeah, but what can I do about it?"

"Exactly what you're doing. Talk about it." Murray leaned back in his chair. "You know, after you called yesterday, I ran a check on you. You've got a great record, Sean. But I know what you're going through: one fuckup cancels out years of hearing 'Great job, buddy.' Right?"

Sean nodded, relieved that Murray knew exactly how he was feeling. He couldn't have said it better if he tried.

"Well, I'm gonna try to help you with that. You've taken the all-important first step, which is getting your ass in here and opening your mouth. The rest is gravy, relatively speaking."

"I'm having trouble sleeping," Sean confessed.

"That's common, too. Don't worry: I won't let you walk out of here without some coping techniques. You familiar with deep breathing? Visualization? Meditation?"

Sean laughed.

"What's so funny?"

"Nothing, it's just that I used to date this girl who was into all that stuff, and I gave her a hard time about it, that's all."

"Well, she was on to something," said Murray, "but the key will be finding what works for you. Every guy in the department for any length of time has gone through what you're going through right now at one time or another. Anyone who says otherwise is a liar. Now, why don't you tell me about the fire."

•   •   •

The next morning, Gemma was eager to get to work so she could do some research on the *cimaruta*. How long had Nonna been wearing it, hidden under her clothes? She already knew each of the charms hanging from the three branches of the tree had a specific meaning—she just couldn't remember what they were. Now, fired up by the possibility that the beloved matriarch of the family might turn out to be a keeper of the "old ways," Gemma wanted to learn everything she could about the two-sided medallion. She felt like a soldier loading up on ammunition; the next time her mother decided to get on her case about being a witch, Gemma would be able to turn to her and say, "So's your own mother, and here's proof."

Spending twenty-four hours with Nonna had been more exhausting than Gemma had anticipated. Sometimes Nonna was her old devilish self, and they laughed. Other times the simplest task—like remembering how to hold a fork—overwhelmed her and she became irascible. At 3 A.M., Gemma heard her rooting around in the kitchen and got downstairs just in time to stop Nonna from going out the back door into the freezing night with nothing on but her nightgown. To keep a better eye on her, Gemma spent the rest of the night in the other half of the ancient, lumpy bed. She didn't get much sleep; Nonna seemed to be more agitated at night. Luckily, by the time Gemma's mother arrived to relieve her, Nonna had exhausted her stores of energy and was sleeping soundly.

So Gemma was tired but in good spirits as she turned onto Thompson Street. But her mood changed when she saw Uther and three other men in medieval garb standing outside her store. Uther was wearing his chain mail and a pewter helmet that looked like an inverted soup bowl, his his left hand gripping a tall halberd. The other men were in burgundy tights and leather jerkins. One had on a metal skull cap; the other two wore felt caps with long trailing feathers. Each of Uther's chums boasted a quiver of arrows on his shoulder. Gemma contemplated turning around and running but it was too late: Uther had spotted her and was waving madly.

Plus she had a business to run.

"To what do I owe this pleasure?" she said mildly, regretting her phrasing immediately. She *should* have said, "What's up?" Now Uther was bound to address her as if they were starring in *Camelot*.

"I wanted you to meet some of my reenacting companions, good lady. They are eager to meet you, as I've told them great tales of your tarot prowess. But I thought if you could see us in our Agincourt garb, you might be tempted to come to our next meeting. We're in sore need of damsels to rescue—"

"Or camp followers," added the man in the skull cap, leering.

Gemma had no idea what a "camp follower" was, but deduced it couldn't be good, if the deadly look Uther cast his way meant anything. She nodded, trying to be polite. "Do you have any literature I could take? That would be helpful."

Uther tapped the side of his head. "It's all here."

Great, Gemma thought, putting the key in the lock. "Well, I'll think about it. Thanks for stopping by. Bye now."

She pushed open the door, expecting them to disperse. Instead, they followed her inside.

"Uther, what are you doing?"

"I want them to see the store."

Gemma pinched the bridge of her nose. "That's fine, but if you guys are going to browse, I suggest you put your weapons behind the counter."

"Why?"

"Because they might scare the customers."

"Oh."

Uther and his friends dutifully followed Gemma to the

counter, stashing their arms for safekeeping. Gemma was beginning to wonder if Uther had a screw loose. As his friends fanned out across the aisles, talking to each other in a way that set Gemma's teeth on edge ("Methinks I see a book on fairie lore!" "Forsooth, a soft chair to set my botty upon!"), Gemma tugged lightly on Uther's chain mail, holding him back.

"How was your date with Frankie?" She hadn't had a chance to speak with Frankie yet.

"A gentleman doesn't kiss and tell."

"You can tell a little. Did you have fun? Are you seeing each other again?"

"Aye," Uther revealed, looking pleased.

Gemma's heart lightened. "I'm glad," she said, giving his arm a little squeeze as he walked off to join his friends.

She didn't mind them being in the store, but when one potential customer entered and left, then another, then a third, she knew she was going to have to ask them to leave. The buying public apparently was not entranced by chain mail, skullcaps, and jerkins. It did make her wonder: As weird as those fleeing the Golden Bough perceived Uther and his friends to be, was that how her mother perceived her?

She had felt the first hint of the worst headache of her life minutes after letting Uther and his friends into the Golden Bough, but had thought it would go away when they did. She was wrong. By the time her part-timer, Julie, came in to work at five, Gemma knew she was going to have to hit the nearest Duane Reade and get herself some aspirin. She hated putting anything like that in her body, but this headache was *bad.* How on earth did Theresa deal with migraines? The relentless hammering on Gemma's temples gave her newfound respect for Michael's wife.

Exhausted, in pain, she pushed open the heavy glass

door of Duane Reade. The lighting was harsh and artificial,
the narrow aisles crowded with shoppers. Directed to the
pain relief aisle by a sullen teen whose baggy pants looked
on the verge of falling off, she found herself confronted
with rows and rows of similar-looking boxes, all promising to soothe this ache or relieve that spasm. Didn't anyone take plain aspirin anymore? It took a while, but she
finally found it, on the shelf nearest the floor.

Clutching her precious booty, she made for the front of
the store, dismayed to see only one cashier behind the register. Taking her place in line, she closed her eyes. *Please,
Goddess, don't let this take too long. I just want to take my
drugs and crawl in bed.*

She opened her eyes, resigned to spending the next fifteen minutes in the crowded, overwarm store. Desperate to
pass the time, she studied her surroundings. That's when
she saw it: the FDNY Calendar for 2006. With Christmas
right around the corner, all the calendars for the upcoming
year were out and on display.

Telling herself it was nothing more than curiosity, she
plucked the nearest one from the rack and began thumbing
through it. The firefighter selected for the month of Febru-
ary was cute enough; blond and buff, he was the "can man"
for an engine company on the Upper East Side. The April
guy didn't do it for her, though. He was too sculpted, too
perfect, a Ken doll come to life. She flipped through May,
June, July, and then, shockingly, she hit August. Her heart
jolted: The firefighter featured was Sean.

Heat swam to her face as she studied the image of the
man who had wooed her so vigorously, only to give up at
the first hint of difficulty. The photo didn't do justice to the
piercing quality of his blue eyes. Nor did it adequately cap-
ture his crooked, boyish grin. But that was his body, all
right. The very same one that had embraced her so tight
and moved so fluently inside her. Choking back tears,
Gemma abruptly closed the calendar.

"Can I see that?" the woman on line behind her piped up. "That guy was hot."

Gemma handed over the calendar and turned back to face the front of the store.

Once upon a time, she would have viewed stumbling across Sean's image in the calendar as an omen. But she no longer believed in omens or coincidences or even fate. It wasn't that she didn't want to; she couldn't afford to.

It hurt too much.

CHAPTER

17

"No offense, but what are you doing?"

Sean slowly opened his eyes to find JJ standing in front of him, staring worriedly. He was sitting alone at the table in the firehouse kitchen. JJ had stopped by at the end of his shift so they could grab a bite to eat.

He unclasped his hands, smiling up at his friend. "Deep breathing. Relaxing." Just as Dan Murray had recommended, when he was feeling stressed, Sean now closed his eyes and concentrated on his breathing. Miraculously, it seemed to be helping. He could actually feel his heartbeat slowing down, the tension in his shoulders fading. Gemma hadn't been kidding: Alternative stuff really *worked.*

"Jesus Christ, you look like you died sitting up. Since when did you aspire to swamidom?"

"Since I went to talk to the counseling unit about the brownstone fire."

"You did?" There was no mistaking the relief in her voice as she waited for him to rise and put on his leather jacket. "Do you think it helped?"

Sean picked his words carefully. "It seemed to." He wasn't yet ready to say so definitively. But Dan was right about one thing: Talking about it helped. The Kennealy household might have functioned a helluva lot more smoothly if there'd been a counseling unit back when his father was still dragging hose.

"Where we going?" JJ asked, following Sean out the door.

"I need to stop by my apartment to check on Pete and Roger. Is that okay?"

"Sure."

"What are you in the mood for?"

JJ looked hopeful. "Italian?"

He shrugged. "No problem."

"That's what I love about you. You're so easygoing."

The irony of JJ's words struck him a few minutes later as they stepped off the elevator in his building's lobby and ran smack into Gemma. He felt tongue-tied and awkward. Concerned, too: She looked exhausted; her soft brown eyes were ringed with circles, the airy bounce in her step conspicuously absent. Was he the cause? Guilt engulfed him.

"Hi," he said, straining to keep his tone light and casual.

"Hi." Gemma's placid face was all politeness. Her eyes flicked to his friend. "Hello."

JJ nodded, smiling. "Hello."

Sean turned to her awkwardly. "Would you mind giving me a minute?"

"Sure." JJ threw him an odd look before smiling again at Gemma. "Nice meeting you."

Gemma's eyes were downcast. "You, too."

As JJ walked to the front door, Sean felt sick. He wanted to spill his guts, here, now, tell Gemma everything he'd learned from talking to the counselor; apologize, beg her to give him another chance, make her laugh till her eyes lit up again and there was color in her cheeks. Instead he stood there paralyzed, watching as she moved toward the elevator.

"Gemma?"

Her expression was wary as she turned back to him.

"Are you all right? You look a little pale."

"I'm fine. I just have a bad headache, is all."

"There must be an herb for that. Or something."

It was the right thing to say. Her mouth almost curled into a smile. Almost.

"There is. Feverfew."

"Is that what's in the bag?"

He knew he sounded like an idiot, but he didn't care. He wanted to keep the conversation going. He wanted to keep her here until he figured out how to say what needed to be said.

Gemma rattled the bag. "Aspirin."

He nodded. What could he say to that? How much? What kind? Ah, aspirin, yes, that always works for me? She was looking at him a bit oddly now. Could he blame her? It was none of his business what was in her bag.

He nervously licked his lips. "Well, um, I hope you feel better."

"Me, too." She turned to the elevator.

Well, that's that, Sean thought glumly. *Opportunity blown, over and out.* Then she abruptly turned back to him.

"I'm sorry. I didn't ask how you were."

"Fine, fine." Sean nodded vigorously. Nothing like a good lie to get the heart racing. *Keep nodding, keep smiling.*

"I'm glad," Gemma said quietly.

Maybe it was the headache, but Sean thought she looked distinctly pained as she stepped into the elevator, though she was doing her best to hide it.

"Have a nice night, Sean."

"You, too," he said as the elevator doors snapped closed in his face.

And . . . cut! That's a wrap. Frowning, Sean zipped up his jacket and went outside to meet JJ. He knew women; she'd want to know "what that was all about." JJ would probably tell him he was an idiot not to seize the moment. Sadly, he agreed with her.

"*Do you think* I'm a jerk?" Sean asked abruptly.

He and JJ had just given their order to a waiter named Dodge. As predicted, JJ wanted to know all about the woman they'd run into in the lobby. As Sean filled her in on all the facts, JJ listened attentively and a battle raged inside his head over whether or not he was a fool not to have made better use of the encounter. A larger question ate at him as well: If he missed her so much, why didn't he apologize and try to get back together with her? That's when he had blurted out his question.

JJ smiled politely at the waiter as he placed their salads before them. "Can I get Sir or Madam anything else before I depart?" he asked, clasping his hands behind his back.

"This is fine, thanks," Sean said, watching him go.

"Why would a mother saddle a child with the name 'Dodge'?"

"You think that's his real name?" Sean said with disbelief. "Get a grip. He's probably an actor."

"No one trying to break into show biz is going to take the name 'Dodge,' believe me." She reached for the pepper. "Now, what was your question again? Do I think you're a jerk?"

"Yeah."

"In general, or does this have to do with a specific situation?"

"Specific. Specifically Gemma."

JJ looked uneasy. "I thought so. You've been distracted ever since we ran into her."

Sean poked at his salad. "I miss her."

JJ swallowed nervously. "Sean, I have to tell you something, and you have to promise not to get pissed."

"Okay."

"That woman—Gemma? Your ex-girlfriend? She, um, stopped by your apartment that weekend I was bird-sitting."

Sean felt the bottom drop out of his stomach. "She did?"

"Yeah. I forgot to tell you."

"And—?"

"This is the 'Don't get pissed' part."

Sean's fingers tightened around his napkin. "Okay."

JJ's words tumbled out in a rush. "She came to the door and I opened it and I was wearing your robe and she asked for you and I was on the phone fighting with Chris and I just said 'He's not here right now' and I closed the door and forgot all about it until now. I'm sorry."

Sean made a sound like a dying moose and covered his face with his hands. "Oh, shit."

Eventually he uncovered his face, staring in disbelief at JJ. She sank down lower in her seat.

"I really wish you'd told me sooner, JJ."

"I know. I'm so, so sorry, Sean."

Sean sighed. "It's not your fault. Well, it is, but there's nothing I can do about it now." His fist hit the table, making JJ flinch. "Shit!"

"There is something you can do about it," she said tentatively. "Go talk to her. Tell her you miss her. Beg her forgiveness and ask her to go out with you again."

"I can't."

"Why not?"

"Because the woman clearly hates me. She could hardly stand talking to me. Now I know why."

"I thought you said she asked how you were?"

"She did."

"Women don't ask how you are if they wish you were dead."

"You don't know Gemma. She's nice to everyone. Bin Laden could step into the elevator beside her and she'd try to talk him out of jihad. That's the kind of person she is."

"I don't know what to say. You cut her loose, and now you want her back. There's only one way to make that happen: Apologize."

"Yeah, but—"

"But what?" JJ asked softly. "It's not rocket science, for God's sake."

"No, but it is complicated." He grimaced. "I don't know if you could tell by seeing her for those few seconds, but Gemma's not exactly a typical firefighter's girlfriend, you know?"

JJ looked appalled. "What the hell does that mean?"

"I told you about that night we went out with some guys from my house. It was a disaster."

JJ put down her fork. "Okay, let me make sure I'm getting this straight. You miss Gemma, but you're hesitant to get back with her because a few of the boneheads you work with think she's a little offbeat?"

"I guess," Sean muttered.

"Then you *are* an idiot."

"Gee, thanks."

"You wanted to know what I think; there it is. No offense, but who the hell cares what those guys think of Gemma? It's what you think that matters."

"They'll give me shit, JJ. They already have."

"Then give it back to them! We all give each other shit about everything anyway! If it's not Gemma, it'll be something else. This is ridiculous, Sean. Are Leary and those other yahoos the ones you're going to come home to after a long day's work? Are they going to give you a family?

Grow old with you? I know you worked hard to get them to accept you, but you succeeded, Sean. Any hell you catch from here on in is just bluster. And if it's not, then I think you need to get yourself some new friends. Life's too short to screw around with this stuff," she concluded in a choking voice.

Sean thought her food had gone down the wrong pipe. Then he realized: She was starting to cry.

"Hey." His hand snaked across the table to hers. "You okay?"

"Ignore me," she sniffled, waving him away. "It's PMS."

"Bull."

"Okay, it's not. It's me and Chris. If Gemma makes you happy, go after her."

"I don't know if I can give her what she wants. Not right now, anyway."

"Then offer what you can and see what she says. If she tells you to get lost, at least you'll know you gave it your best shot." Swiping at her eyes, she glanced frantically around the restaurant. "Now where's Dodge? I need a glass of water."

"Excuse me, Janucz?"

Sean tried not to feel embarrassed for the building super as he jerked awake at the sound of Sean's voice. Janucz had been snoring so loudly Sean had been able to hear him all the way down the hall. He wasn't surprised, therefore, when he arrived at the super's tiny basement office to find him with his feet up on the desk and his head lolling on his chest.

"Sean, Sean, how are you?" The burly Pole motioned for Sean to come through the doorway. "What can I do for you?"

"A favor. A big one."

"For you? Anything."

Sean smiled at the compliment. The staff and the other tenants in his building loved that a firefighter lived under the same roof. They thought it somehow made them safer. Sean had never traded on his status, but there was a first time for everything.

"I need you to go into 5B when the tenant isn't home and put this inside." He reached outside the doorway and grabbed a large, wrapped box.

"What is this?" Janucz asked suspiciously.

"A present."

"And you want Janucz to place it in 5B? Falconetti?"

"It's not Falconetti anymore, but yeah."

"Why for?"

To his surprise, Sean felt mildly embarrassed even discussing it. "It's a surprise. For the woman who's living there now."

"Yeah?" Janucz wriggled his eyebrows suggestively. "That little redhead in 5B? She is your special friend?"

Sean feigned a wolfish grin he knew would communicate better to Janucz than words. "She was. I want her to be again. That's why I need you to put this in her apartment. I want to surprise her."

"Hhmm." Janucz folded his hands across his soft belly, and tilted back in his old office chair. "This is illegal, you know, just going into someone's apartment for no reason. Janucz could get in trouble."

"I know." Sean felt badly, compromising this kind soul. "But it's for a good cause. And I could pay you," he added.

"You pay nothing," Janucz shot back, sounding insulted. "You are a great hero of this city."

Yeah, right, Sean thought. But to Janucz he simply said, "Thank you."

Janucz looked up at him with earnest, narrowed eyes. "If I do this for you, do you swear to tell no one, not even you own mother?"

Sean crossed his heart. "I swear."

"You swear on the grave of you father?"

Exasperated, Sean bit the inside of his cheek. "My father's still alive, Janucz. But yes, I swear."

"All right." Pitching himself out of the chair, Janucz leaned forward and, picking up the box, put it on his desk. "Let me see . . . 5B, 5B, 5B," he muttered to himself. Then: "Oh, shit."

"What?"

"You know who live on that floor? Croppy." He shook his head sadly. "Sorry, Sean. Too dangerous."

"Croppy won't be a problem," he assured Janucz.

"What? Are you crazy? Croppy's always problem. Her late husband? Beelzebub, I'm telling you. He's the only one who would have her."

"Listen," Sean said patiently. "It's none of her business why you're going into Gemma's apartment with a gift box. For all she knows, Gemma asked you to bring it up for her."

"Hhmm." Janucz rubbed his pocked chin. "You are right, Sean. But if Croppy sees me, she will bust my balls. You know this. But I will do this for you anyway."

"Thank you." Sean couldn't express his gratitude enough. "Gemma usually leaves for work at around eight, and is home between six-thirty and seven. Can you do it tomorrow?"

"I can do it. No sweating," Janucz said proudly.

Sean patted Janucz's shoulder. "I really appreciate this."

"No sweating," Janucz repeated. "You are a great hero of this city."

A day later the encounter with Sean still had Gemma rattled. It was too much, seeing his image on the calendar and then running into him in the lobby minutes later with his new girlfriend in tow. It felt like a cruel sensory over-